A WRIGHT CHRISTMAS

A WRIGHT CHRISTMAS

K.A. LINDE

ALSO BY K. A. LINDE

WRIGHTS

The Wright Brother ✦ *The Wright Boss*

The Wright Mistake ✦ *The Wright Secret*

The Wright Love ✦ *The Wright One*

A Wright Christmas

CRUEL

One Cruel Night ✦ *Cruel Money*

Cruel Fortune ✦ *Cruel Legacy*

SEASONS

His for a Season ✦ *The Lying Season*

The Hating Season ✦ *The Breaking Season*

RECORD SERIES

Off the Record ✦ *On the Record*

For the Record

Struck from the Record ✦ *Broken Record*

AVOIDING SERIES

Avoiding Commitment ✦ *Avoiding Responsibility*

Avoiding Temptation

Avoiding Extras ✦ *Avoiding Boxset*

DIAMOND GIRLS SERIES

Rock Hard ✦ *A Girl's Best Friend*

In the Rough ✦ *Shine Bright*

Under Pressure

TAKE ME DUET

Take Me for Granted ✦ *Take Me with You*

STAND ALONE

Following Me

Paranormal Romance

BLOOD TYPE SERIES

Blood Type ✦ *Blood Match* ✦ *Blood Cure*

Young Adult Fantasy

ASCENSION SERIES

The Affiliate ✦ *The Bound*

The Consort ✦ *The Society*

The Domina

ROYAL HOUSES

House of Dragons

For my mom,
who loves Christmas romance novels
and encouraged my love of dance.

1

PEYTON

*S*ixteen years, five months and twenty-seven days.

That was how long it had been since I'd gotten into the summer intensive in New York City and left Lubbock, Texas, behind forever for the sprawling, bustling world of professional ballet. I never thought sixteen years, five months, and twenty-seven days later that I would be back in Lubbock. Not for any dance-related reason at least.

"Peyton, over here!" My sister, Piper, waved enthusiastically as I stepped through the revolving door with my dance bag and carry-on tucked tight to my side.

"Pipes!" I called, dashing through the crowd as if it were New York City streets.

"Don't call me that," Piper cried. She threw her arms around me but not before I saw her roll her eyes.

"Someone has to keep you on your toes."

"Ugh! And here I thought, I was happy to have my sister home for the holiday season."

I released her with a laugh, pressing back one of my

loose curls into the braided bun at my head. "You are happy."

"Yeah, yeah," Piper said, ignoring her own brown hair.

She'd gotten lucky with our mom's thick, stick-straight hair. Straight hair would have been much easier than my father's curls that went back to his proud Mexican heritage. All of our aunts and uncles had hair like me, which I couldn't deny I loved, but straight hair would have been better for ballet buns.

"Let's go get your luggage."

"I'm good." I gestured to my small carry-on suitcase and dance bag, which currently contained a dozen new pointe shoes, an equal number of leos and tights, as well as enough tape wrap, toe pads, and sewing materials to make it through a season of *The Nutcracker*.

Piper eyed my scant luggage. "You know that you're going to do something other than dance while you're here, right?"

"Not if I can help it," I said with a smile.

"All right, fiiine," Piper grumbled. She knew the shtick too well by now. "Let's go, seester."

We exited the Lubbock airport and stepped out into the dry, arid climate that was my home. Having grown up in the middle of nowhere West Texas, I'd gotten really good at disabusing people of their biases about what Lubbock was like. No, it was not technically a "small town." Unless you considered three hundred thousand people small. Small compared to New York City, not to what most people thought of when they heard the words *small town*. Yes, we had cowboys, but it was really just a city like anywhere else. People wore their hats, boots, and pressed jeans as their Sunday best, but no one was riding their horses into town. Okay, only that one time, and everyone had taken pictures because it was weird, y'all. Fine, most of the town was a cotton field and as flat as a pancake, but it was still home. Tumbleweeds and all.

We reached Piper's blue Jeep, as bright as a spotlight in the sea of black and white trucks. The words *Sinclair Cellars* were plastered on the side.

"How's the winery?" I asked, dumping my bags into the back.

"As excellent as ever. Dad thinks we're going to have a new vintage this year, a specialty blend that's going to win us awards." Piper beamed.

When I was little, the only thing that I'd known other than ballet was the vineyards at Sinclair Cellars. Our dad had worked there his entire life, starting at the lowest job and moving all the way up to the top. So, when Ray Sinclair finally decided to retire, my dad had taken over. His kids still weren't particularly pleased.

Piper worked at the winery full-time. She had a real knack for it.

"That's great," I told her, dropping into the passenger seat.

She revved the engine and then gunned it out of the airport.

"And Peter?"

"With his boyfriend," Piper said.

"Probably for the better. I have to head to the studio as soon as I get in."

As much as I wanted to see my brother, Piper's twin, it would have to wait.

"All right. You can probably borrow the Jeep."

The Jeep. Right. I'd have to start driving again. I'd gotten really used to walking everywhere I needed to go, occasionally taking the subway or a taxi. I was going to have to reacquaint myself with driving.

"Maybe I should rent a car," I said, which wasn't something I'd considered before this moment.

"Nah. Dad's probably already figured something out for you." She veered onto 27 South and headed into town. "Mom wanted to have a tamale marathon for your first day back."

I groaned.

"But I convinced her that you'd be too jet-lagged to helped make, let alone eat, seventy-two tamales."

"Thank God."

"I'm just so glad your home for what feels like...ever."

I laughed. "It's only for a month."

"A month. You haven't been home for more than a few days in over a decade."

"I know."

And I did, but I had a demanding job.

It had been hard enough to balance life and dance when I lived here. I'd made time for Isaac, and that was about it. My heart panged when I thought about him, and I forced myself to look out the window as we passed through Piper's neighborhood.

Isaac Donoghue had been my first everything. My first love, my first kiss, my first...time. He'd taken my heart wholly and completely, and I wasn't so sure that he'd ever given it back.

I hadn't seen him since that day sixteen years ago when I got on that plane to make my dreams come true. He'd encouraged it, even convinced me to go to New York. I couldn't say I regretted it, but I still wished that there had been a way to have both.

Now, I was going to be home for a month, and our circle was too small not to run into him. A quick smile darted to my face in anticipation. Would it be so wrong to *hope* to see him again? Even if I knew nothing could come from it? He had his own life, and mine was back in New York.

But he was still Isaac Donoghue. The boy who had changed my life. The boy I had loved unconditionally. The boy who had let me go.

"Here we are," Piper said, killing the engine once we were in front of her one-story white brick house in Tech Terrace. She'd gotten it for a crazy steal right out of college and spent the last six years renovating it. It helped that her on-again, off-again boyfriend, Bradley, had work part time in college for Wright Construction, the biggest construction company in the US.

I carried my dance bag inside as Piper carted in my suitcase.

"You'll be in the back bedroom on the right. Blaire recently abandoned it for the bonus room because she— quote—*needed the natural light for her Instagram pictures.*" Piper shrugged. "Anyway, it has a connected bathroom."

"Thanks, Piper. I appreciate you putting me up. Your house is way closer to the studio than Mom and Dad's."

"Yeah, I should have considered that when buying this house. It would be convenient to be farther south, so I'd be closer to the winery," she contemplated. "But at the time, I was only thinking about proximity to the bar scene."

I snorted. "And since when has that changed?"

Piper grinned. "It hasn't."

"Okay, I'm going to get ready. You're sure I can use the Jeep? I don't mind catching an Uber."

Piper waved her hand, already walking into the kitchen and popping the top off a Mexican Coke. "By all means. Blaire should be home soon, and if there's an emergency, I can always ping Bradley."

"Are you two still a thing?"

"No," Piper said. I arched an eyebrow. "What? We're friends."

"Uh-huh," I muttered and then headed into the back room to change.

After being in travel clothes all day, it felt right to get back into tights and a leotard. Sleep beckoned after such an early flight, but I had my fitting for the Sugar Plum Fairy costume, and I couldn't miss it.

I put street clothes over top of my dance garb, grabbed my bag, and then headed out to the Jeep. It took me a few minutes to get used to the hulking beast of a car. I'd learned to drive on my dad's hooptie—a truck that took too much force for me to be able to open the driver's side—so I always crawled in from the passenger. This should have been easier than that old hunk of junk, but it was still intimidating. After carefully backing out in the road, I got the hang of it and drove to the new Buddy Holly Hall downtown.

With the creation of the new performing arts center, the Lubbock Ballet Company had moved from their long-time space on 34th Street, where I had first been introduced to ballet, into the new facility. I was anxious to see the building, which had been modeled off of the NYC Ballet studios that I was used to. A slice of the city in my hometown.

I parked out front of the massive complex and ambled in through the studio entrance. The artistic director, Kathy Brown—who had just been a budding director when I danced here as a kid—was supposed to meet me here, but I was still a few minutes early. I headed down the row of studios. My heart soared when I saw the enormous rooms with ballet barres lining the floor-to-ceiling glass windows that faced equally large mirrors. This did indeed feel just like home. Most of the rooms were empty, save for a baby ballet class taught by a high school–aged student. I continued forward until I found what I was looking for.

In the studio were a handful of advanced students—one Black girl at the front with her partner, a fair-skinned young man with red hair and freckles; a Latina girl gossiped in the back with two white girls; and another brown male dancer stood off to the side, idly doing *rond de jambes* on the floor. Honestly, I was surprised there was this much diversity. When I had been here, I'd been one of the only non-white dancers.

Kathy stood at the front of the room, heavily pregnant but still lithe and moving with ease around the studio.

The couple started again, and my eyebrows rose. I hadn't expected to be impressed, but watching the girl at the center, I only saw potential.

Kathy clapped her hands, ending the rehearsal, and came out to find me. "Peyton! I'm so glad you're here."

"Kathy, it's so good to see you," I told her, drawing her into a hug.

"I can't believe I finally convinced you to be my Sugar Plum Fairy. It is going to be so amazing to watch you on that stage again."

I smiled at her. "And look at you," I gushed. "Going to have another ballerina?"

"God willing," she told me. "Don't worry. She's not due until Christmas. We'll make it through the next month together."

I laughed, and my eyes wandered to the company members who exited the studio, landing on the Black dancer once more as she trailed the other dancers, who clustered together like a unit. "She's really good."

Kathy nodded. "Too good for here," she said wistfully. "Bebe is only in high school."

My eyebrows rose. "High school? You mean, this isn't the professional company?"

"Nope. Just my pre-professional. Katelyn Lawson, her understudy," she said, pointing out a tall, trim blonde, "has already been accepted to Joffrey for the summer. Bebe doesn't think she's ready. She's only been dancing for two years."

"Oh my God, Kathy," I whispered.

"I know." Kathy patted me on the arm. "Don't worry

about the company. I'll keep working on her. She's a little prodigy, just like someone else I know."

I flushed. Even after dancing professionally for fifteen years, hearing that word—*prodigy*—made my heart leap. "Thank you, Kathy."

"Now, come. Let's get you fitted."

I followed Kathy into the costume room, happy to fall back into the old, familiar feeling. When I'd decided at seventeen to move to New York, I'd left so much behind —this town, my family...Isaac. It felt almost *right* to be here again as my career wound down.

2

ISAAC

"**Y**ou wanted to see me?" I said, sticking my head into Jensen Wright's all-glass office.

Though Jensen Wright Construction was technically a separate entity from Wright Construction, in practice, they were one and the same. Jensen running the architecture and his younger sister Morgan working as CEO of the construction side. The best and the brightest of the Wrights came together in the largest construction company in the nation.

"Isaac, yes. You got my email?" Jensen glanced up from his twenty-seven-inch computer monitor.

"Sure did."

"Come on in. This will be quick."

I stepped inside, securing the first available seat in front of him. Jensen was the oldest of five, and after his parents had passed, he had all but raised many of his younger siblings. The Wrights had a ten-year age gap between Jensen and his youngest sister, Sutton, with Austin, Landon, and Morgan in between. Even though I'd grown up with Landon and known Jensen my entire life, I couldn't help but idolize him. I was thirty years old and still saw him as the too-cool older brother I never had.

"You might have heard rumors about a new facility Wright Construction is working on," Jensen said.

I nodded. There were always rumors. "A sports team is coming here?"

"Since we have Tech, it's normally just petty gossip. Everyone wants a Minor League Baseball team or the like to come to Lubbock, but it never pans out."

"Right, because we're not on a major highway. Highway 27 doesn't connect all the way down to 20, and we're smack between 20 and 30."

"Yeah, well, that's all about to change," Jensen said confidently. "Last week, Wright Construction got the green light to build a soccer facility for a Division II professional league."

My jaw dropped open. "Seriously? That's...incredible. I never thought that would happen in Lubbock."

"Honestly, neither did I," Jensen agreed. "But since I know you have the most experience with the sport and my architecture company is running the design specifics, I want to get your input on design, and Morgan agreed to put you in charge of the project team."

I nodded enthusiastically. "Yes, of course. I'm happy to help."

I'd been recruited all over the country for soccer right out of high school and played two years of DI soccer at Southern Methodist University in Dallas. But nothing had really panned out like my dreams had always hoped they would, and I'd quit the team before my junior year, moved back to Lubbock, and graduated from Texas Tech. I still had mixed feelings about the whole thing.

"Excellent. We're in early stages, of course, but let's put you on the books for all the main planning meetings with me, Morgan, David, and Jordan."

"Will do."

I could just imagine myself in a room with all the most important people at Wright. Morgan, CEO of Wright Construction, was a total badass at her job. David had come in from San Francisco to be our newest CFO. And Jordan was a Wright cousin. He and his father had been in charge of the Canadian division of the company, headquartered in Vancouver, but he had moved down to Lubbock with his mom and younger brother three years ago. He was a total shark, and I could see why they wanted to bring him in on this new project.

And while I'd worked my way up at Wright straight out of college and been the project lead on the new Buddy Holly Center downtown, this felt different somehow. I wasn't just implementing what others had created. I was in the room where it happened.

I stayed in Jensen's office for the next hour, going over everything that I would want to include in a professional soccer stadium. Of course, we already had a baseline for what we had to include, but the Wrights never did anything half-assed. So, this had to be the biggest and best.

"God, is it already four thirty?" I asked, checking my watch. "I have to get out of here. I have to pick up Aly."

Jensen leaned back in his chair and laughed. "I do

tend to get a little carried away. Emery is probably going to want me home at some sort of reasonable hour today."

"That seems likely. When is she due?"

"Not until the spring."

"Well, congrats, man," I said, shaking his hand. "Do you know if it's a boy or a girl?"

He sighed heavily. "Girl."

I tried to cover my laughter at his dismay. "You're going to do great. Girls are easy."

He raised an eyebrow. "I don't think anyone can say children are easy."

"True."

"Well, get out of here. I'm going to finish this up."

I tipped my head at him and headed out the door. I was probably going to be late. Again. I dashed across the parking lot and into my truck. My mom usually picked Aly up from school and took her to the studio, but I was responsible for picking her up after work. I didn't normally get caught in philosophical discussions with Jensen Wright.

Luckily, no cops caught me speeding through down-town Lubbock to pull into the Buddy Holly Center parking lot. I'd actually managed to arrive two whole minutes early. I loosened my tie and tossed it onto the seat next to me, unbuttoned the top button of my shirt, and ran a hand back through my auburn hair. Good enough.

With a sigh, I exited my truck and headed inside the Lubbock Ballet Company's studio. Aly had been dancing here for the last three years. Everyone thought I was crazy for putting her in ballet at only two years old, but honestly, the kid had come out dancing. She cried if she didn't go straight to the studio after school. It felt a bit like a curse to me, but she loved dancing so much, so how could I ever deny her?

The lobby was full of parents that I recognized from Aly's classes. I tipped my head at a few of them. I knew basically everyone in the city. In my line of work, it was hard not to know everyone. But it was Angelica and Bart Lawson, Lubbock's resident high-profile lawyer team, who approached me. Kill me now.

"Angelica," I said with a head nod. I took Bart's hand. "Bart."

"Isaac, just lovely to see you," Angelica said.

"You too."

"How's Aly?"

"You know Aly. Always happy to be in dance tights." I laughed with the couple. "How's everything going with Katelyn?"

Angelica pursed her lips. "Well, they gave the Clara role to Bebe."

She made it sound like it was an affront. I knew enough about ballet to know that Bebe was the best dancer we'd seen in over a decade. My heart panged at that thought. Being here always reminded me of Peyton. I tried to hide it all away, but there was a reason I knew how the ballet world worked.

"They should have given it to our Katelyn," Bart said.

"She's worked so much harder for this," Angelica agreed. "Don't you think so?"

There was no winning here. I couldn't say that Bebe was the better dancer. Katelyn did work hard, but she had the added advantage of parents who cared *way* too much.

"What part is Katelyn playing?" I asked instead.

Angelica waved her hand. "She's a soloist in the snow scene, and she's one of the flowers. But it's not the same as being Clara, especially the way that Kathy choreographs the role."

"Of course. Those are both great parts." I glanced over their shoulders. The baby class hadn't let out yet. "Excuse me. I'm going to go check on Aly."

I brushed past the couple and headed toward the studio space. Just as I was nearly to Aly's class, Kathy stepped out of the costume room with another woman.

I stopped dead in my tracks, my stomach dropping to the floor. It couldn't be. This made no sense. I was having a hallucination. That was the only possible explanation for this. Because what would Peyton Medina, a principal dancer in New York City, be doing in Lubbock?

But there was no denying it.

No one else had her grace or poise. The slicked-back bun that had wisps of brown curls constantly escaping, no matter how much hairspray or gel she applied. The lithe frame with her tan complexion. The dimple that appeared just on her right cheek when she really smiled, as she was now. The widening of her big brown eyes as she saw me for the first time, too.

"Isaac?" she gasped.

Her eyes swept up and down my form, just as I had done to her. Something ignited inside me. She'd left so long ago, and still, that connection between us sparked. I took a half-step forward for a moment, remembering all the times I'd held her perfect body and kissed her perfect lips.

Before I ripped myself away from who we'd been at seventeen and back to the present, an ache settled in its place. An old, familiar feeling of missing her. One that had never truly gone away.

"Hey, Peyton."

3

PEYTON

*I*saac Donoghue was standing in the Lubbock Ballet Company lobby.

I blinked and blinked again. This wasn't going away. He was really there. Right there. As if I had conjured him out of thin air. I'd anticipated seeing him but not on my first day back. Not here, like this, where I was so unguarded.

God, I had been so hopelessly in love with him. And looking into those green eyes, I could see it happening all over again. Just how easy it would be to get lost in my first love.

He was somehow even more gorgeous than I remembered. He towered over me, as he always had. And while he'd been tall and lanky in high school with his intense soccer schedule, plus running cross-country, he had completely filled out. His shoulders were broad and defined in his suit, his waist tapered in, and his chest had expanded considerably. But it was the bright green of his eyes, the red scruff along his defined jawline, and the warmth of that smile that had always drawn me in. Just as they did now.

"Hi," I said, flustered.

He laughed softly, and something in my chest eased at the sound. "It's good to see you. What are you doing in town?"

"I'm...well, Kathy invited me out to perform as the Sugar Plum Fairy for the season."

Kathy deviously grinned at us both. "We're so lucky to have her. If you'll excuse me..."

"That's incredible," Isaac said. "You're not performing in New York?"

"I rearranged my schedule to dance the last week of the year in New York so that I could be here for the entire LBC *Nutcracker* season."

"Wow. So, you'll be here for a month?"

I nodded. A whole month...and Isaac was here.

He stepped forward, shedding the distance between us. Fire shot through me.

"That's amazing. I'm sure your family is glad to have you home."

"They are," I said at once, fidgeting with the loose curl at my temple that I still couldn't get into place. I dropped my gaze and then lifted it to his again. I wet my lips. "I thought we might run into each other."

"Oh yeah?"

"Kind of a small circle."

"True."

"I just...didn't guess it'd be on my first day," I said with a small shrug.

"Yeah, what are the chances? So, you just got in?"

"Yeah, Piper picked me up from the airport. I'm kind of beat, and I'm still supposed to have dinner with Peter and my parents."

"Oh, well, don't let me keep you."

"You're not," I insisted, a faint blush touching my cheeks. "I just mean...this is nice. It's good to catch up with old friends."

Something shifted in his face.

Friends. Why had I said friends? What was I even thinking?

"Sure. Definitely. It's been a long time."

I wanted to say more. Being around him felt...right. It always had. Fate had twisted us together again. Could I even deny that I'd wanted it to?

"It has."

"Do you need a ride or something?" he asked, always the gentleman.

"Oh, no. I took Piper's Jeep. I'm sure she's counting down the minutes until I bring it back. You know how she is."

He laughed. "I do. I was just surprised to see you."

Me too.

Just looking at him, I could tell that it had been so very long since I'd seen him. We weren't teenagers anymore. Things had changed. And ballet still stood between us...as it always had.

He seemed to be willing to let me walk right by and out of his life again. And for a second, I decided that I didn't want that.

"Maybe we should meet up," I blurted out.

My blush only deepened. There was no reason *not* to

get a drink with Isaac. We hadn't seen each other in sixteen years. It wasn't like I wanted to start a relationship or anything. I was going back to New York in a month anyway.

"Sure," he said with a half-smile. "My number hasn't changed."

I swallowed. "No. Mine hasn't either."

"Then, call me or send a text. We can figure something out."

"I'll do that."

His smile never wavered.

Then the door to the baby ballet room opened, and a surge of little dancers in pink tights and leos and skirts came bounding into the lobby. A smile crossed my face at the excitement on all the little dancers' faces. I loved this moment. Not all, probably not even very many, of these little ones would make it past the next couple of years. But for the few who loved dance so much that it was in their very bones, they'd keep dancing. And it was in their faces that I saw myself and boundless opportunity. Any one of them could be the next star.

"Daddy!" a little girl with ginger-red hair screamed as she rushed toward Isaac.

My heart stopped.

I hadn't even wondered what Isaac was doing in the lobby of the ballet company on a Thursday afternoon. It didn't even occur to me. I'd been so dumbstruck by his presence that I didn't even consider his real reason for being here—he had a daughter.

"Aly Cat!" he cried, scooping up the little girl and

pulling her in close. He covered her face in kisses until she squealed with delight.

And as much as my heart ached to see it, it also glowed. Isaac was a great father. Just as I'd always known that he would be. My own disappointment clouded my mind.

For a second, I was seventeen again and standing at a crossroads. In one direction was everything I'd ever wanted—New York City, principal ballerina, dancing in front of thousands in Lincoln Center. And in the other direction was Isaac, a family, a life. I'd chosen one, and standing before me now was the other. But it wasn't my family or my life. He had made that with someone else. As he had every right to.

I stepped back, a lump forming in my throat. I was happy for him even if, outwardly, I struggled to show it. He deserved a beautiful child and wife and the life he'd always dreamed of for us. But it didn't hurt any less.

"Aly, let me introduce you to an old friend of mine," Isaac said, swinging the little girl around. "*This* is Peyton Medina."

"Hi, Peyton," Aly gushed, wiggling out of Isaac's arms to stand next to me. She only came up to my hip, but she was full of energy. "I've heard all about you. You're a ballerina. A *real* ballerina."

I startled out of my own melancholy. "You've heard about me?"

"Of course! My daddy only knows one real ballerina. One day, I'm going to move to New York and dance on a stage, just like you!"

I squatted down to her level. "I believe that you will."

"Of course I will. Daddy tells me that I can be anything I want when I grow up."

"He's right."

"I'm even going to be a mouse in *The Nutcracker* this year."

"That's quite impressive," I encouraged. "And how old are you?"

She held her hand out. "Five. But I'm going to be six in April."

"Wow. That is quite an accomplishment for a five-year-old."

"I know. I'm smart and a good listener," she boasted.

I cracked a smile.

"And modest, too," Isaac said with a laugh, ruffling Aly's perfect ballet bun.

"Dad, don't mess up my hair!"

"Do you want to know something, Aly?" I asked.

She nodded vigorously.

I tried not to laugh. "I am going to be the Sugar Plum Fairy in *The Nutcracker* here in Lubbock this year."

Aly screamed in delight. Isaac shushed her with an eye roll as the parents who were still nearby looked over in shock. "That is going to be ah-may-zing! Daddy, did you hear?"

"I did, Aly Cat. Now, you should probably let Peyton go. I'm sure you will see her around a lot at rehearsals."

"I can't wait," she said, clenching her hands into fists and shaking with joy.

I straightened up and hauled my dance bag back over my shoulder. "Well...I'll see you around."

Isaac nodded at me. "Looking forward to it."

I swallowed back my disappointment and all the questions I wanted to ask. First and foremost among them: *Where's her mom?*

I was deeply regretting not being on social media. For so long in my career, it had meant direct access to my critics, and I just hadn't been able to handle that. Now, I was wondering how I could be so out of the loop.

With one more backward glance at Isaac holding Aly's tiny hand, I hastened out of the Lubbock Ballet Company lobby and away from all my what-ifs from the past.

4

PEYTON

"**Y**ou will never guess who I ran into at the Lubbock Ballet Company," I said to Piper later that day as I drove with her and Blaire to my parents' home on the south side of town.

"Isaac Donoghue," Piper guessed.

My eyes widened. "How did you guess?"

"Because his daughter is obsessed with dance. She's there almost every day."

"What?" I gasped. "You knew this and didn't tell me?"

"Everyone knows that, Peyton," Blaire said from the backseat.

I turned around to glare at her, but Blaire just laughed. She was Piper's roommate and best friend from college. They'd been inseparable ever since they first met. She had a baseball hat low over her wide blue eyes, and her nearly black hair whipped around her face in the wind with the Jeep's top down. It was too cold to have the top down at the end of November, but Piper always liked to push boundaries.

"Well, I didn't know that. It was quite a shock to meet his daughter."

"She's so cute though, isn't she?" Piper said.

"She is. Is her mom...in the picture?" I asked as nonchalantly as I could.

But Piper's smile fell off her face. "She died...in childbirth."

"Oh."

I flushed and looked out the window as the streets of my parents' neighborhood zoomed past. Christmas lights dotted the houses as everyone prepared for the upcoming holiday. For so long, that had only meant extra hours in the studio and endless *Nutcracker* performances. Not that I'd ever minded. But in that moment, I minded.

"Yeah, he's doing okay now, as far as I know," Piper said. "It was pretty traumatic at the time."

"I can only imagine." With a sigh, I turned back to Piper. "So, he's a single dad? Not...attached?"

Piper's smile returned. "Are you interested?"

"No," I said automatically. "I'm only here for a month. I'm just trying to digest everything I missed."

"Liar."

Blaire cackled from the backseat. "Yeah, he's single. His parents and sister help take care of Aly a lot."

"Oh, wow, Annie," I said, remembering his sister's name. "I haven't seen her in forever. She was just a little kid when I left."

"She's in med school now," Piper said.

"That's amazing."

"Yeah, Blaire plays on Isaac and Annie's soccer team, the Tacos."

"The Tacos?" I asked with an eye roll.

"Hey the Tacos are awesome!" Blair said. She leaned forward. "Anyway, Isaac started the team. He's so much better than the rest of us, but I try to keep up. Julian and Hollin aren't bad, but they're not as good as me." She got a wicked glint in her eye. "You could come with me on Sunday. It's indoor."

"Oh no, I couldn't do that," I said immediately. "I mean, it would be weird, right?"

"What's weird is you trying to deny that you're still into Isaac," Piper said as she pulled up to our parents' house.

I ignored her...even if she was right. Especially because she was right.

Instead, I chose to marvel in the splendor of the Christmas display. Every year, my dad tried to outdo himself on Christmas lights. Already this year, he had every inch of the house plastered in lights, and a few of those inflatable Christmas displays were up and operational. He'd recently gotten into adding music and synchronizing the lights display with his favorite songs, which ranged from "All I Want for Christmas Is You" to "Despacito." The videos they sent always made me laugh.

Piper parked out front, and we hopped out of her Jeep. She jogged around the hood to meet Blaire and me as we walked up to the front door. My brother's SUV was parked in the driveway. He opened the door before we could even knock and barreled into me, picking me up and twirling me around.

"Peyton's home!" Peter called inside.

"Pipe—Pey—Peter!" our mother, Hannah, called,

always messing our names up. "Whatever your name is, put your sister down right this instant and go help your father with the spaghetti."

Peter set me down with a wink. He and Piper were so similar sometimes, it was terrifying. They were twins, though Piper would proudly proclaim that she had been born three minutes earlier. And they even looked alike. Same straight dark brown hair and chocolate eyes with a proud, defined jawline and golden skin. Only Peter was a good head taller than both of us.

"You know, Mom, you wouldn't mess up our names so much if you hadn't named us so similarly."

"Bah," she said, waving a dishrag at me as I stepped inside. "I still would. As long as I get the person right on the last one, that's all that counts."

I let her pull me into a hug and kiss my cheek. "I missed you."

"I missed you, too. But at least we'll have you for a month this year. That's more than I can ask for."

"It's good to be home. Where's *Abuelita*?" I asked about my grandmother.

"She couldn't make it tonight, but she's anxious to see you. You should swing by her place when you have time."

"I will. If I have time."

Peter's boyfriend, Jeremy, was already seated at the dinner table with a copy of *The Great Gatsby* in his lap. He was an English PhD at Tech and could always be found with a book close at hand.

"Jeremy," I said, and when he didn't look up, I repeated his name.

He blinked rapidly and glanced up, completely lost in his book. "Did you say something?"

"I was just trying to say hello."

He smiled and tucked *Gatsby* under his arm. He stood to his considerable height, six and a half feet tall and as lanky as they came. Fair as could be—as if, like a vampire, he never saw the sun—with blond hair that always fell forward into his baby-blues and a disarming crook of his lips. Like he wasn't quite used to looking people in the eye. He was the opposite of my brother, but they just seemed to fit.

He shook my hand. My family were huggers. I wondered how he survived it.

"Good to see you again."

"You too," he said, then promptly sat back down and continued reading.

"Mom, do you know who Peyton ran into today at LBC?" Piper asked from the kitchen.

I groaned and hurried toward the sound of Piper's annoying voice.

"Isaac Donoghue," Piper announced before I could stop her.

Everyone turned to look at me when I stepped into the already-crowded kitchen.

"What?" I grumbled and snatched a fresh-baked roll off of the plate that my dad had just taken out of the oven. It was too hot though, and I tossed it back and forth between my hands until it cooled down.

"Isaac is such a nice young man," my mom said, nudging her husband. "Don't you think so, Matthew?"

My dad caught my gaze. His eyes crinkled when he

looked at me. He set the plate down and came over to pull me into a hug. "I'm glad you're home, pumpkin."

"Me too, Dad."

"Well, anyway," my mom continued, "I think he has such a cute little kid. Did you meet Aly?"

"I did," I confirmed. "She was adorable. I can't believe she's going to be a mouse in *The Nutcracker* at only five years old."

"Why? You were," my mom reminded me.

"Yeah...but..."

Piper laughed. "Not everyone is a prodigy?"

"That wasn't what I was going to say."

Peter and Piper exchanged *the* look. I threw my roll at Piper's face. She gasped when it hit her, and then she bent down to pick it back up and hurl it at me. But my father wrenched it out of her hand.

"I spent hours on those. Let's not throw them at each other," my dad said.

"Well, now, it feels like Peyton's home," my mom said with a sigh. "You three are incorrigible."

"The spaghetti's ready. Everyone grab something and take it out to the table," my dad said, hustling us out of his kitchen.

Though my mom loved to make traditional Mexican food that she had learned from her mom and grand-mother, she was a terrible cook otherwise. She claimed it had something to do with her great-grandmother's recipes having magic in them. But otherwise, Dad cooked. When he had still been working his way up at Sinclair Cellars, we'd eaten a lot of takeout, but every Sunday, we would sit down for a real home-cooked meal.

Just the smell of my dad's secret spaghetti sauce brought back so many childhood memories.

I picked up the basket of rolls and followed my mom and siblings into the dining room. I set them down next to Piper's plate since I knew she would eat more than the rest of us combined, and with my father's metabolism, she'd not gain a pound. A feat I still didn't understand.

Once everyone served themselves, my mom said grace, and then we dug in. But still, Piper wouldn't let the thing with Isaac go.

"So, are you going to go out with him?"

I stuffed my mouth full of spaghetti and shot her a death glare.

My mom just laughed. "What about you and Bradley?"

Piper shrugged and picked at her salad. "We're just friends."

"That's what they call it nowadays," Peter said from the other end of the table.

"Hey!" Piper snarled.

Peter laughed. "What? You can give it but not take it?"

"I think Isaac is a good man," my dad said thoughtfully. He looked at Piper with a raised eyebrow. "Better than this Bradley fellow."

Piper sighed heavily. "I know, Dad. This is why we're friends."

Blaire snorted. Piper elbowed her in the arm.

My dad met my gaze. "I know you're only here for a month, pumpkin, but a lot can happen in a month."

I gulped and nodded. My dad always had a way of speaking to me thoughtfully. Even if he said the exact same things that everyone else said that made me cringe. "I know."

"Blaire invited her to the Tacos soccer game this Sunday," Piper volunteered. "Isaac's team."

"You should go," my mom said.

"No, I still think it would be weird," I said quickly. "We don't know each other anymore. We haven't even seen each other in sixteen years."

My dad glared at Piper to keep her quiet, and the conversation veered toward other topics—Piper's new idea for the winery; Blaire's new job, teaching Pure Barre; and Peter's latest comic book find. I was glad to be left out of the conversation.

There was no way that I was going to go to Isaac's soccer game. I'd mentioned that we should meet up, and he'd said I could text him, but that was before I knew he had a daughter. That changed things. I didn't want to get into his life for a month, only to leave again. Not when he had someone else's feelings to think about.

I wasn't going to text him. And I wasn't going to go to his soccer game. That was settled.

5

ISAAC

"*W*here even is your head at tonight?" Annie asked from the passenger seat. "We're going to be late."

"We're not going to be late," I told her.

We probably were. Since having Aly, I was late almost everywhere. I used to be the kind of guy who thought fifteen minutes early was on time and on time was late, but, man, kids changed all of that.

"I mean, you usually run behind now but not for soccer."

I shrugged and took the next turn north toward the indoor complex. "I guess my mind is on other things."

"Like?" Annie prodded as she finished French-braiding her dark red hair.

"Peyton."

Annie's eyebrows rose. She tied off the completed right side before turning to face me. "Peyton Medina?"

"What other Peyton do we know?"

"I don't know. It's been a few years since I've heard that name out of your mouth."

"Well, she's back in town."

"What?"

"Just for the month. She's performing as the Sugar Plum Fairy in *The Nutcracker*."

"Did you see her? When did this happen?" Annie asked excitedly.

"I guess Thursday. I ran into her when I was picking up Aly."

"And you're just now telling me this?"

I rolled my eyes at my sister. "I haven't even seen you since Thursday."

"Yeah, I'm in med school. You never see me, but pick up a phone or something, dude. What are you going to do?"

That I didn't know. I knew what I wanted to do. I wanted to ask her out. I wanted to take her out to dinner and hear all the amazing things that she had accomplished since she left Lubbock and me behind all those years ago. I wanted things to be what they had been.

But...I knew that was impossible. Nothing could go back to the way they had been. She'd left, and I'd told her to. I couldn't stand between her and her dream. Not when I'd had such high hopes for my soccer career. I wasn't the same person either. First and foremost, I had Aly to think about. As much as the kid adored anyone who danced and would surely idolize Peyton, would it be fair of me to introduce her to Peyton when I wanted more? Would it be fair to any of us?

Lots of questions and no answers.

I pulled into the parking lot and killed the engine in front of the indoor complex. Annie and I hopped out and grabbed our soccer bags out of the bed of the truck.

"You need to get her out of your head, or you're not going to be able to play tonight," Annie told me.

"I know. I mean, I told her she could call or text me. She said that we should meet up. But I haven't heard from her in four days. That probably means I'll never hear from her, right?"

Annie slung her bag over her shoulder. "You haven't seen her in sixteen years. Seems unlikely you'll see her again if she didn't text you the next day."

I nodded and pulled open the door to the soccer facility, letting Annie step inside first. "You're right. I'll just put it out of my mind. No reason to dwell on the past."

"Or not," Annie muttered, frozen in place.

"Or not?" I asked in confusion.

Then, I stepped inside.

Peyton Medina was seated in the bleachers.

"Oh," I whispered.

God, I'd forgotten how beautiful she was. Thursday, when I'd seen her still in tights and a leotard, it was like nothing had changed. Sixteen years had just disappeared. But now, she sat on the bleachers in street clothes, next to Annie's friends, Jennifer Gibson and Sutton Wright, and I was a goner. Simple jeans and a white sweater with her wild, curly hair out of its immaculate bun shouldn't have done me in, but it did. And I wanted nothing more to go over there and kiss her.

"Earth to Isaac," Annie hissed. "She's waving."

I raised my hand and waved back.

"Go say something to her, you idiot."

The first buzzer rang then, announcing five minutes until game time.

"There's no time. We have to go warm up."

Annie rolled her eyes. "You go. I'm going to say hi."

True to her word, Annie raced off to the bleachers, waving at her friends and then crushing Peyton in a hug. I wanted to go over there, but five-minutes already wasn't enough time to warm up. Not if I wanted to win this match...and I did. My competitive streak was unparalleled.

I dropped my bag at the bench and put on my shin guards before jogging up and down the sidelines. I interspersed high knees and some side shuffles before returning to the bench. Annie was stretching next to Blaire, who grinned broadly at me.

"You're welcome," she said.

"What's she talking about?" Hollin Abbey asked.

I'd played soccer with him on an intramural team at Tech. He was a solidly built white guy. With how big he was, I was sometimes surprised that he was the fastest guy on our team.

"Nothing."

"Doesn't seem like nothing, does it, Julian?" Hollin asked.

Julian glanced up with an amused look on his face. It had come as a shock to me to learn that Julian Wright, cousin to Jensen, was also Hollin's cousin on his mom's side. Small towns were weird. But at least it meant we got another good player. Julian was built more like me with the same fair skin and clever footwork. He'd kicked ass on a rec team in Vancouver.

"Blaire does seem awfully smug," Julian offered with his award-winning Wright smile.

"I am smug," Blaire said. "I got his high school sweet-heart to come watch him play."

"Ohhh," Hollin said. "Is she hot?"

"Can we not?" I asked.

Annie giggled from where she was warming up. "You had this one coming, bro."

Thankfully, the ref blew the whistle for game time. I shook hands with the rest of our team who had just finished warming up and gave a quick pep talk before sending everyone out to their positions. Blaire played forward because girls' goals counted as two. It was half the reason we were destroying the rest of the teams this season. Blaire ran circles around the competition. Julian and I played midfield, and Hollin, with his bulk, defended alongside Annie and Cézanne—a tall, quick-footed player with her signature box braids, who Annie knew from medical school. Our goalie, Gerome, was even taller than Hollin with locs for days and miracle hands. He'd only missed a handful of balls all season. I was confident that we could take the title this season.

It was a pretty fair spread, and I wasn't confident in the win until Blaire landed the last goal. Hollin was a bit of a ball hog and liked to score even though he was supposed to be defending. He and Cézanne got into it a lot. Julian was sometimes too cautious, but overall, we were getting the hang of playing as a team.

We shook hands with our opponents after we beat them and then headed back to the bench.

"Great game, everyone," I told them. "Keep this up, and we're going to win the season."

"Pizza?" Hollin asked the rest of the team.

I groaned. I couldn't imagine eating a slice of pizza right now. "I'll pass. I need to get home to Aly."

The rest of the team agreed and arranged to meet at Capital Pizza since they were one of the few late-night pizza joints still open.

Annie nudged me. "I'm going to get pizza with Jennifer, Sutton, and Blaire." She winked. "Don't wait up."

I shook my head at her. "Annie..."

She held her hands up. "Hey, I'm just saying. Mom and Dad have Aly. She's probably already in bed. Doesn't hurt a damn thing for you to have a little more time to yourself for once."

She had a point. And she knew it. Because she just grinned wider and ran after Blaire. "Hey, wait up!"

After throwing my shin guards back into my bag and taking a long drink of water, I shouldered my bag and headed over to where Peyton sat.

"Hey, good game," she said at my approach.

"Thanks. I was a little nervous there at the end."

She laughed, and something skipped in my heart. I had missed that sound. "I know how competitive you are. There was no way you were going to let them beat you."

I shrugged and dropped my bag. "Well, it doesn't always work out."

"No, I suppose not," she agreed. "Jenny and Sutton said something about going to get pizza." She tugged on a curly lock and let it bounce back up. "It feels a little weird, even saying those words. I haven't seen some of these people in years, and they act like I just belong among them."

"You do," I said automatically.

She shrugged. "No, I don't. But it's nice of them to include me. Were you going to get pizza?"

"No, I can't imagine eating a slice after all that. Not to mention, the beer consumption Hollin manages. Plus, I have to get home to Aly."

Her face fell slightly at the words, and I kicked myself for saying them. Annie had just told me to live a little. That Aly was fine for the night. Maybe I was the one who didn't belong in this world. I certainly wasn't used to having a night to myself.

"But not quite yet," I added quickly. "If you want to maybe get some ice cream?"

She hopped down off of the bleacher, a tentative smile coming to her face. "My kryptonite, Donoghue."

I grinned. Didn't I know it? "Is that a yes?"

"Yes."

6

PEYTON

*S*ince Blaire was heading out for pizza, Isaac drove us to Braum's. He parked the truck out front in the already- full parking lot.

"What's happening here tonight?" I asked, gracefully sliding out of the passenger side.

"Nothing. Just the normal high school crowd."

I arched an eyebrow but followed him inside and immediately saw what he meant. The restaurant was packed with high school–aged kids sitting around with ice cream cones and gossiping like their life depended on it.

"Is it always like this?" I asked as we got in line.

"Pretty much."

"Huh. We used to go to Holly Hop," I said before I thought better of it.

He froze momentarily, and then the tension disappeared. "Holly Hop is all the rage. Probably still my favorite ice cream in town, but Braum's is open later, and their ice cream is affordable."

"Hence the high school crowd."

"Yep."

The frenzied worker stepped up to the counter. "Has someone helped you?"

"No. I'll take a single scoop of chocolate chip cookie dough in a waffle cone."

"Got it." She looked to Isaac. "And you?"

"A scoop of chocolate-toffee and chocolate-chunk chocolate cheesecake in a chocolate waffle cone."

The woman dashed away to prepare our orders. I couldn't help but laugh at him.

"You didn't want pizza, but you ordered *that*?"

"Hey, ice cream is always a good idea."

"Confirmed," I said with another laugh.

I hadn't laughed like this in...years. I had friends in the city and, of course, all the women that I danced with, who I loved. We had a good time, but it wasn't this. It wasn't Isaac.

"Plus, chocolate is the flavor of life. Aly inherited that gene from me, I'm afraid. When we come here, she always ends up with chocolate smeared all over her face."

I giggled. "I could see that. She seems like a precocious kid."

"You have no idea." He glanced away. "Sorry to keep bringing her up. I'm sure that's not—"

"Hey, don't do that. I haven't seen you in sixteen years. If you didn't talk about your kid, I'd think there was something wrong with you."

Isaac nodded thoughtfully and then took the ice cream offered. He stepped forward to pay, but I got in front of him.

"I can get mine," I said quickly.

I didn't want him to think this was a…date. Or anything. He didn't have to pay for me.

But he scooted me to the side with an eye roll. "It's three dollars, Pey. I think I can handle it."

I opened my mouth to object, but he'd already tapped his credit card. And that was that. Well, all right then.

We took our ice cream to the very back of the restaurant, farthest away from the crowd of rowdy teenagers. Another family seemed to have the same idea. They sat in silence against the windows as "Last Christmas" finished playing, and the Pentatonix version of "Hallelujah" trickled in through the speakers.

I nibbled on my cone as Isaac devoured his. It felt strangely reminiscent of old times.

Ice cream had been our first "date." We'd both been freshman in high school. The very first week of school, Isaac approached me and asked me if I wanted to get ice cream. We'd gone to different middle schools, and I had no idea who he was. But he did it in front of *all* of my friends, and I was too embarrassed to say no. Who was this kid with this much self-confidence?

Well, it had turned out to be a dare. Not that it made the ice cream date any less wonderful.

Our parents had dropped us off at Holly Hop that weekend, and he insisted on paying. We got to know each other and found that we had a lot in common. We liked the same TV shows, we read the same novels, we both had athletic aspirations, and, well, he was *really* cute. Monday, when we got back to school and I found out the whole thing had been a joke, I cried in the girls' bathroom and vowed never to date again.

We all know how well that went. He'd sent a letter that said he was *really* sorry and asked if I'd be his girlfriend with little squares underneath it to check *yes* or *no*. I'd checked yes...and the rest was history.

"So, what happened with your soccer career? I know that you wanted to play professionally. I'm not on social media or anything, so I haven't kept up with anyone's life."

I didn't say that I'd avoided his life in particular. Thinking of him after I'd left was too hard.

"Well, not much to tell, honestly," he said after he finished his bite of ice cream. "I went to SMU for two years on scholarship. The first year, I loved it. I was getting recognized by scouts for the MLS, and I even spoke to a training group for Barcelona." He shrugged. "But then SMU got a new coach for my sophomore year, and we...didn't see eye to eye."

"Ugh!"

"Yeah. He stopped starting me. My prospects dwindled. It was a year of turmoil and so...I left. I couldn't stick around and be hamstrung by a coach who had killed my chance at doing this full-time. I transferred into Tech and played on their club team. It wasn't the same, but I got my degree, and I work for Wright now."

"Wow. I'm so sorry, Isaac."

He waved me away. "That was a long time ago. I'm fine with it now. If I'd taken a different path, then I might not have Aly, and she's my life."

His face glowed when he talked about his daughter. It

made something in my chest tighten.

"Did you...meet her mom at Tech?" I asked carefully.

He looked up in surprise.

"Piper told me what happened."

"Ah...that makes sense." He finished off his cone with one final bite. "Abby and I met at SMU actually. She was from Dallas, and her brother was on the soccer team. When she graduated, she moved to Lubbock to work for Wright. We met up again at work and hit it off. We got married and had a kid, and then she was gone."

Without thinking, I reached across the table and grasped his hand. "That must have been devastating."

He gave me a wan smile, squeezed my hand back, and then withdrew it. "It was. It was pretty rough at the time. My parents helped a lot. They still do actually. Abby's parents live in Dallas, and they help out when they can. But they're not here, so it's different." He shook off the sadness that had washed over him and returned to his regular self. "That was five years ago, and I'll never regret having Aly. She's the best thing that's ever happened to me."

"You're lucky to have her."

"I haven't had much luck in my life, but if I did, then she would be it." He laughed and ran a hand back through his red hair. His green eyes were bright when he made eye contact with me again. "Enough about me. Tell me about you. I might or might not have seen that you were dating someone in New York. Some famous ballet dancer?"

I flushed at the words. "You've been keeping tabs on me?"

"Peyton, your life is sometimes chronicled in celeb mags, and you had a piece in *Time* magazine."

"Oh God," I said, covering my face. "You read that article?"

"Don't be embarrassed. It was great. I would have never known that you had a career-threatening injury without it. It's a miracle that you're even dancing right now."

He wasn't wrong. I cringed at the thought of the start of last season when I'd been performing the lead for *Giselle* and something in my knee popped. To this day, I had no idea how I'd finished that show. But I hadn't been allowed on pointe again for six months. Six. Months.

I'd thought my career was over. But after intense rehab, I was finally back full-time again. Who cared that my knee still screamed after every performance? A ballerina knew only one truth: your days as a dancer were limited. I intended to use every one that I had.

"I forget sometimes that everyone knows about in my life. I didn't even want to do that *Time* article. My friend Macy works there and kind of hassled me into it. I really would prefer to be more private."

"You get the good with the bad. You followed your dreams. You are the principal ballerina that you always wanted to be."

"You're right," I said quickly. "I don't mean to sound ungrateful. I love my job. I am so lucky to still be dancing full-time at thirty-three."

"You don't sound ungrateful, and we both know it isn't luck. It's a lot of hard work," he insisted.

"True. I am in the studio constantly right now. Especially with the rehab on my knee. I started working with a personal trainer after I got out of physical therapy to try to build up the muscles so that I could compete against eighteen-year-olds again. It's been an uphill battle." I looked down and bit my lip before continuing, "As you can imagine, *more* time in the studio isn't exactly conducive to dating. I was already there eight, nine, sometimes ten hours a day. With the extra PT and training, well, I'm sure you can imagine. Serge and I just sort of ended during that."

He scoffed. "You were busy trying to get your career back. That doesn't sound like the time to give up on a relationship. It sounds like the time you needed someone to be there more than ever."

A knot formed in my throat at the words. Those perfectly placed words that I hadn't realized I needed to hear until he said them. I had needed someone during all of that. And instead of staying, Serge had vanished.

"It was for the better," I finally said when I could get my voice under control. "Serge and I started dating when we both made principal in the same year. It went well for a while. We moved in together. Then it became ...convenient." I shrugged. "It was ending anyway. We were both just too busy to say it. Then, when I got injured, it was the excuse he needed."

It was Isaac's turn to reach forward and take my hand. "That wasn't fair to you. He should have been there."

I waved him away. "It's fine. Really. Ancient history. I've been better without him."

Before we could say anything else, a group of the high schoolers burst into song in the corner. I jerked at the sudden rendition of "Rockin' Around the Christmas Tree." A beatboxer joined in, and a Latina girl began to belt out the chorus.

"Do you suddenly feel like you're in a bad musical?" I asked Isaac.

"Totally. They're not that bad though."

"I think that's the Frenship High School a cappella group. The main girl is wearing their T-shirt."

He laughed as the crowd cheered the end of the song, and they launched into another one. "You want to get out of here?"

I nodded. "I don't know if I can take much more of the random bouts of singing."

We hastened out of Braum's and back into his truck. I shivered as I waited for the heater to kick on.

"You know, I could call an Uber if you wanted to get back to Aly sooner," I offered.

"Don't be ridiculous. I'm not going to abandon you to find your own way home."

"I've lived in New York, Isaac. I think that I can find my own way home."

"That's New York. You're in Texas now."

He put the truck into drive, and that ended the argument. It was only a ten-minute drive back to Piper's house.

"Thanks for the ride home," I said gratefully.

"Anytime, Peyton."

I flicked the lock and stepped out of the truck. Then, I dipped my head back inside. "It really was good to see you again."

He smiled, and for a second, I thought about getting

back into that truck and being seventeen again. Putting the car in park and making out in the driveway until it was past curfew. But that was a different Peyton and a different Isaac.

"It was great to see you, too, Peyton. Don't be a stranger."

"I won't. Night."

I slammed the door shut and began to head up to the front door. But then, before I got there, I jogged back to the driver's side. He rolled down the window with raised eyebrows.

"Can I help you?"

"Well, there's an LBC charity event on Wednesday before the first show on Friday night. We're giving an exclusive sneak peek of the cast, plus drinks and appetizers. I didn't know if you might be interested in coming. I can get you a ticket."

"And I'd get to see you dance?"

I nodded once.

"I'll have to figure out what to do with Aly, but...I'd like that. It's been a long time since I've seen you dance."

I beamed, all the while chiding myself for inviting him at all. "Well, great. I'll...I'll see you there."

"Sounds good. Night, Peyton."

"Night, Isaac," I said softly before walking back to the house.

For the first time in a long, long time, I felt as light and airy as the characters I portrayed onstage. I didn't know what was happening with Isaac and me. I didn't know if it was even smart to do it. But for once, I didn't care.

7

PEYTON

"Seeing you in a tutu just makes me all teary-eyed," Kathy said, waving her hand in front of her face. "Or maybe it's the hormones."

I chuckled and pulled Kathy in for a quick hug. "You're just nostalgic."

The Sugar Plum Fairy tutu had finally been finished and fitted with my measurements yesterday, but we weren't doing a full-dress rehearsal for the Open Barre charity event tonight. I was currently in a plain white tutu along with the rest of the ensemble cast, who I had been rehearsing with for nearly a week. It wasn't like dancing with my family back at New York City Ballet, but I fit in just fine.

Thankfully, most of my role was the solo "Dance of the Sugar Plum Fairy" and my *pas de deux* with the Cavalier. Both were the traditional Balanchine choreography, which I had danced hundreds of times. So, the most important part had been extra hours in the studio with my partner, Reginald, to perfect the duet.

Cassidy, the production manager, tittered energetically in the wings. She was a longtime feature in the studio. When I had been dancing at LBC with her daughter, Beth, she had just been a stage mom, but she had worked her way up over the years. She ushered about the high school students, moving them into formation. Kathy waddled after her to talk to the lot. I could see their nerves from here.

Reginald came to my side with a smile. He was fair-skinned with dark hair and eyes. Not as good as the men I was used to performing with, but he was solid. His girl-friend was also in the company, and I knew she was sad that she hadn't been given the role of Sugar Plum Fairy beside him. Ah, the challenges of dating in a company.

"Ten minutes," Kathy announced to the crowd of dancers. "They're all filing into the auditorium now. Places, everyone."

I bustled into the wings beside Reginald.

"Good luck," he whispered.

I almost laughed. This wasn't a real performance, of course. Just a staged rehearsal, but the exhilaration right before getting onstage hit me all the same. "You too!"

I pranced up and down on the box of my toe shoes, stretching out my arches and calves, rolling through the hard shank on the bottom of the slipper that held to the shape of my foot. This was my twenty-eighth year of dancing in *The Nutcracker*. I had started as young as Aly and continued every single year in my career. It was the cornerstone of my dance performances. I didn't know a single dancer who had performed the same dances more than in *The Nutcracker*. During performance weeks, when we were doing two-a-day shows, I would still hear "Waltz of the Flowers" in my dreams.

The curtain rose, lights flickered to life, and Kathy stepped onto the marley floor to a round of applause. A minute later, she was introducing us. I held my arms in front of me as I gracefully ran out onto the stage along with the other dancers. I took my mark on stage right and waited beside Reginald.

Kathy moved us through what would appear to be a regular rehearsal schedule, focusing first on the difficulty we were having with the Arabian couple.

"One more time through, Amanda," Kathy said evenly. "Use your whole body in the lift this time. Let Mateo guide you rather than forcing it."

Amanda nodded along with Kathy and then tried it again. I was glad that I was onstage and couldn't cringe because it was definitely worse the second time. They were going to get it by opening night, but they weren't quite there yet.

"Peyton," Kathy said after Amanda was on the ground once more, "do the *pas de deux* lift with Reginald. Everyone, watch her form to see what I mean."

I stepped into position, too used to being an example to feel flustered, even here in front of the eyes of an audience. Kathy counted us in on a *five, six, seven, eight*, and then I was moving. My limbs an extension of my body. I knew Reginald would be there for the leap, and I launched effortlessly into the air. He lifted me with my arms overhead, legs in a split.

"See how Peyton appears to be light as air? Look at the placement of her hands, the strength of her point, the tilt of her head. Every aspect of her is incorporated into that movement. She isn't fighting Reginald on the lift. He's the base, the support. She trusts him and herself."

I landed back on my feet to a spatter of applause. She made Amanda go one more time, and this time, she *was* better. Not quite there, but she'd gotten the dynamics back into place. I'd seen them perform it better in studio than they were today. They just needed to get the kinks out before they went onstage.

"Okay, places, everyone. Let's run through 'Entry of the Parents' in Act I."

I wasn't actually in "Entry of the Parents," but we'd practiced it this week with Reginald and me included in the piece for this event. It wasn't a real struggle. We'd both already known the part. It was just rearranging the partners. The dance itself was a formal nineteenth-century ballroom piece, typically performed in full-length dresses and suits.

Kathy started us all at the midpoint of the dance and counted us in, and then we were off. As so often happened when I danced, everything else disappeared. There was no stage. No lights. No faces watching from the crowd. It was just me doing the thing that I loved most in the world. The job that had chosen me as much as I had chosen it. I'd sacrificed nearly everything in my life so that I could have this. The feeling that coursed through me was indescribable and unlike anything else I'd ever experienced.

Too soon, the dance ended. I was still lost to the exhilaration of the dance as Kathy critiqued the performance. Then, she called for Clara to come forward.

Bebe hastened to take her place, but Katelyn beat her to it. For a second, the two just stared at each other. Katelyn arched an eyebrow in defiance. Bebe ground her teeth together, a flush coming to her cheeks.

The gall of this girl. It took all my will not to tell Katelyn to get back into the corps, where she belonged. But I knew Kathy could handle it.

"Katelyn, I asked for Clara."

"I'm the understudy," she said quickly. "I thought it would be good for me to practice...just in case Bebe can't perform the role."

I sucked in a sharp breath. Well, if that wasn't a threat, I didn't know what was.

Kathy pinched her lips together. "There's no reason Bebe cannot play Clara. None at all. Bebe, step forward, dear. Let's go through the new turn sequence in the middle."

Bebe raised her chin and moved past Katelyn to take her position. My heart was thumping for the girl. I couldn't imagine what Bebe must be feeling. But I sure as hell knew that someone needed to put Katelyn in her place. She hadn't chosen this moment for no reason. She wanted to embarrass Bebe. She'd succeeded, but none of us would forget it either. Kathy was going to have to nip that in the bud before it went any further.

Bebe, to her credit, didn't falter once through the turn sequence. She ended to an even louder round of applause than I had gotten, which was good. She needed the confidence boost and the proof that Katelyn was wrong.

Kathy gestured to all of us. "One more round of applause for our wonderful dancers." Once the audience quieted down, she continued, "There are refreshments in the main lobby after this, and our dancers will be out there to mingle with you. Thank you so much for attending and for your generous support of the Lubbock Ballet Company."

We all ran back into the wings and started for the dressing rooms to get into street clothes for the rest of Open Barre.

"Katelyn Lawson," Kathy snapped, stopping the girl before she could scamper off.

"Yes, Miss Kathy?"

"Here. Now."

Katelyn walked over to the artistic director without fear in her heart. I sure hoped that she learned an ounce of humility from this moment.

I left Kathy to deal with it and changed into a long black romper that tapered at the waist and ankles. I left the ballet bun and stage makeup, grabbed my purse, and went to see if Isaac had ever made it. My stomach fluttered at the thought. I'd been reckless to invite him to this, but I couldn't bring myself to regret it.

But as soon as I walked out, I was bombarded by wealthy donors, some that I recognized from my time with LBC.

"Peyton, you were spectacular," an older gentleman said.

"Yes, we went to see you perform the same role in New York City a few years back, and again, we saw you recently in *Giselle*," his wife said.

"I'm so pleased," I told them. "It's such an honor that you came all the way to the city to see me perform."

"We're huge fans," the man said. "We remember watching you when you were just a little thing. It's been amazing to see you transform."

"Thank you so much."

"Oh, Peyton," another woman in her middle years said, drawing my attention away. "I read that article you did in *Time* magazine."

Oh God, here we go again. I still cursed myself for ever being in that article.

When Macy had approached me about my injury and the work I was doing to recover, I'd thought it would be a fun, easily dismissed fluff piece. But her editor loved it and decided to make it a full four-page spread in the magazine. There was an entire page of just me sitting on the stage at Lincoln Center, putting my ballet slippers on.

I'd done other magazine pieces before, of course. The publicity was part of the job. It helped keep dance and culture and the New York City Ballet in people's minds. But this felt different. This hadn't really been about my dancing; it had been about my biggest downfall. I'd felt vulnerable and exposed. Even though everyone else loved it, I still cringed, thinking about how low I'd fallen.

"It was just incredible, reading about your road to recovery," the woman said. "Truly inspiring."

"Thank you."

"And you're all healed up now?"

I nodded. "Yes, ma'am."

"That's good. I can't wait to see you on opening night."

"Excuse me," a voice cut through my latest flock of admirers.

I turned and found Isaac's handsome face. My heart fluttered. He'd made it.

"Do you mind if I steal Peyton for a minute?"

The woman looked between us with a coy smile on her face. "Not at all." She patted my hand. "It was so nice to meet you."

"You too."

Isaac gestured for me to walk before him, and I did so as quickly as I could without looking like I was scurrying.

"Thank you," I whispered to him.

"For what?"

"Saving me."

He stopped when we were far enough away and met my eyes. "Always, Peyton. Always."

"*A*s much as you love the spotlight onstage, you truly hate it in person," I said to her, grabbing two glasses of champagne off of a passing tray. I handed one to her.

She mumbled, "Thank you," and took a fortifying sip. "Yeah, well, I always have."

"I don't know how you even handle the life you live."

She shrugged. "Most times, I don't know either. But I love ballet more than anything, and it's not always people rushing me to discuss the *Time* article. I should have prepared myself for that."

"You couldn't have known."

She tilted her head to the side and looked off, away from me. Her face was carefully blank, but I could read her like no other. Even all these years later, she gave the same tell. A part of her thought that she should have known what to expect here. She'd always been hard on herself. Perfectionist to the core.

"I'm really glad that you made it," she said instead when she looked back to me.

"I said that I would."

"I know, but you have Aly, and I didn't consider how you were going to get away. This isn't even a real performance or anything."

"Aly is fine. She's with Annie for the night, who was happy to make her go to bed and then study some oversized medical text."

"Well, that's nice of her, but—"

"And I didn't want to miss it, Peyton," I assured her. "You were really amazing onstage."

She flushed and covered it by taking another sip of her champagne. "Thank you. It wasn't much."

"That's not true. You've always been great, but now, you're beyond anything that I've seen. I can tell you've spent years perfecting your craft."

And I wasn't just blowing smoke. Dance brought out something in her. It was a light, a beacon. She glowed onstage, as if there were nowhere else she was supposed to be in the world.

I remembered the first time that I'd seen her dance. Ironically, it was a *Nutcracker* performance. She had been dancing Arabian, and though it was easily the only piece in *Nutcracker* that had any sex appeal, all I saw was a girl who had been born for the stage. A girl that I couldn't live without. It felt dramatic for the time, but I was fifteen years old. We'd been dating for four months, and when she had come out from backstage, I'd told her I loved her.

"Well, I'm glad the years have paid off," she said, modest as ever.

She was on top of her game. What the hell was she doing in Lubbock for the season? Shouldn't she be performing *The Nutcracker* at Lincoln Center all Christmas?

"How did you work it out to be here all month?"

"Oh, I have to be back in the city by Christmas Day to finalize rehearsals, and then I'll dance the entire week between Christmas and New Year's. Most other principals want that week off anyway."

"I'm surprised they agreed to that."

She turned away and waved at a friend approaching. "It was nothing."

But the way she'd said it, the way she couldn't look at me...it wasn't nothing. It was unusual. The old Isaac would have dug his heels in until she told him what was going on. Except I didn't know this Peyton. We weren't the same people, and if she had secrets, well, that was her right.

"Peyton Medina!" a voice cried.

I didn't recognize the brunette heading toward Peyton. She looked like she belonged on a runway rather than in Lubbock, Texas. Her hair had that shiny gloss and huge waves that I knew from growing up with a sister were only achievable from a salon. Her face was a mask of porcelain and ruby-red lips, and she wore a skintight dress on her thin frame and red-lacquered heels—and I was well aware of how expensive they were. It had been Abby's dream to own a pair of Louboutins.

"Oh my God, Katherine?" Peyton said, dazed by her appearance. "What are you doing here?"

"Camden and I came down to see my brother. David married into the Wrights."

Peyton blinked. "Wait, Sutton's husband is *your* brother?"

"Small world, right?" Katherine said with a laugh.

They chatted back and forth rapidly as Katherine's husband appeared beside her. He held his hand out, and I tried not to be intimidated as I shook, but this guy looked like a cross between a duke and a mob boss. His suit probably cost more than my entire wardrobe.

"Camden Percy," he said.

Percy. Shit. I knew that name. He owned the Percy Tower hotel chain. Jesus Christ. Were these the kind of people that Peyton hung out with back in New York?

"Isaac Donoghue," I offered.

"Oh, sorry," Peyton said breathlessly. "Isaac, this is my friend Katherine. We go to the same trainer in the city."

Katherine looked me over once and then nodded at Peyton, as if giving her approval. "Rodrigo is the best, isn't he?"

"Truly. No one compares," Peyton agreed.

Camden stuffed his hands into his pockets and looked put out. "If I have to hear about him one more time..."

The girls burst into giggles. Apparently, this was a common joke.

"Well, we'll be here for another week or two. Give me a call if you do anything fun," Katherine told her. "I still have no idea what to do here. And we'll be at opening night, of course."

"I'll text you," Peyton agreed easily.

Katherine waved at her one more time before tugging her husband away from us. I just stood, dumbfounded. The couple days that Peyton had been home, I had thought that she was mostly the same girl that I'd known before. But...how could I even understand what living in New York had been like for her?

"Wow. That was...Camden Percy," was all I managed to get out.

Peyton giggled, something short of hysterical. "I know. Isn't it so weird? When Katherine first started coming for training with Rodrigo, I thought she was the world's biggest bitch, but she's grown so much in the last year. It's kind of incredible that I'm even friends with someone like that."

It was.

She shook her head. "I never would have expected them to be here. They don't exactly fit, do they?"

"They definitely stand out like a sore thumb."

"They're probably used to galas and Fashion Week and clubbing on top of skyscrapers," she said wistfully.

"And you aren't?"

Her eyes finally snapped to mine. "What? No! Are you joking, Isaac? Do I look like the kind of person who goes to those sorts of things?"

Something in me relaxed at her easy laughter and disbelief. I was overreacting. I'd been worrying that she was too far out of my reach again, but no, she was right here. And she fit in just fine in Lubbock.

I hadn't realized how much stock I'd been putting in having her back until that moment. Until I thought that I had lost her to a glamorous life in the city. But all

Peyton had ever cared about was dance. She wasn't mine to have again. Not yet at least. And I knew that if I lost her to anything, it would be ballet and not some rich socialites.

I laughed with her. "I mean, I guess I didn't really know. It didn't sound like the Peyton I knew, but it has been years."

She shrugged. "I think I'm pretty much the same person as I was. Just more dance."

"And who even knew *more* dance was possible?"

"Always possible." She touched my arm and gestured for us to keep moving. "We should probably mingle."

I nodded and let her lead the way through the crowd of donors of the Lubbock Ballet Company. She was gracious and beautiful through the entire thing. She really did seem more poised now that she was prepared for everyone's attention rather than getting pounced on at the door. It was sort of miraculous to watch her handle the room like a professional. She *was* a professional after all.

Near the end of the evening, Kathy came and hugged Peyton. "Thank you so much for agreeing to do this this season. I wouldn't have wanted anyone else."

"I'm glad to be back," she said truthfully.

Kathy drew me into a hug next. "And always good to see you around LBC. How's Aly?"

"She's great. She can't wait for opening night. I don't think I'm ever going to get her to sleep after she performs. She loves it all so much."

"Sounds like someone else I know," Kathy said, winking at Peyton.

"I do have trouble sleeping after a performance," she said with a shrug.

"Ah, it's so good to see you two in the same place again."

Peyton caught my eye and then flushed, looking away. God, I needed to just ask her out. No more of this tiptoe-ing. I knew that I needed to protect Aly from heartbreak if...*when* Peyton left again. But could I really let her be here in town, where I always wanted her, and *not* make a move?

Kathy suddenly bent over and groaned.

Peyton reached out. "Are you all right?"

"Oh, just...Braxton Hicks," she moaned.

"Are you sure?" I asked carefully.

Peyton looked wide-eyed with fear, but I'd already gone through this once. I remembered when Abby had gone into labor, and it'd looked a hell of a lot like this.

"No," she said faintly. She tried to stifle a cry as another contraction hit her. "They started earlier, during rehearsal. They've been coming on and off. Oh God, I think I'm going into labor."

9

PEYTON

"**N**ot now, baby girl. You have three more weeks in there. It's too soon," Kathy said hoarsely.

"Is there anything we can do?" I asked in shock.

"Get Bryan," Kathy said. "He can drive me to the hospital."

"I'll stay with her," Isaac said, stepping up immediately.

I nodded and dashed across the room to find her husband, Bryan. He was well over six feet tall with a deep brown complexion and a bald head. Everyone always joked that he had more hair on his chin than he'd ever had on his head because he sported a considerable black beard.

Bryan was the orchestra director, and they had met and fallen in love during their very first performance together nearly twenty years ago. It took him a full season before he plucked up the courage to ask her out. They were happily married within the year. It was the fairy tale everyone dreamed of.

"Bryan," I gasped, stopping before him and not caring who I interrupted. "It's Kathy."

"Excuse me," he said to the board members he'd been speaking with. "What's wrong, Peyton?"

"Kathy is going into labor."

He straightened considerably and nodded. "Let's go."

I walked him back over to Kathy, who was now clutching Isaac's hand and drawing a crowd.

"I'm here now, darling," Bryan said. "Come with me, and I'll bring the car around out front."

Kathy nodded, her face contorting into pain. And then they disappeared through their whispering audience.

It wasn't until Kathy and Bryan were gone that I had the realization that no one was going to be around the next month to direct *The Nutcracker*. Kathy having the baby three weeks early meant that there was no artistic director during the most important season of the ballet. My heart sank. What were we going to do?

Cassidy appeared at my side. She looked stunned. "Her other two babies were all late. She thought that she would have a Christmas Day baby."

"Who is going to direct in her place?" I asked.

She shook her head. "I have no idea. We hired an interim artistic director to start in January so that she could take a few months off. But we didn't anticipate needing anyone for the season."

"We should call that person and see if they can come up early."

Cassidy nodded, coming back to herself at being given an order. "Yes. I'll reach out. Though I'm sure she has her own *Nutcracker* to direct. And what are the chances she could be here before Friday?"

I winced. Unlikely. "I don't know."

"God," she whispered. "Well, I'll get to work on it. There's nothing else to be done. The show must go on."

"Of course. If there's anything I can do, just let me know. If you need help with rehearsals, I can run them. I've performed every role. Until the new AD gets here, I can probably get us through to Friday."

Cassidy clutched my hand. "You're a godsend. Thank you. Let me get the schedule together and figure out when we need you. Can you hang around until after this is over?"

"Of course."

Cassidy ran off to coordinate and came back a few minutes later. "Could you do the closing speech for tonight? Kathy was supposed to say a few words. I know it would mean a lot for it to come from you. But if you can't, Nick can."

I swallowed and nodded. It was just another stage. Even if I hated public speaking. "Sure. I can do that."

"You're the best, Peyton."

Isaac raised his eyebrow. "You're going to give a speech?"

I frowned. "I couldn't exactly say no."

He rubbed my arm. "It's going to be fine."

I took comfort in his reassurance, but I sure didn't feel it. I didn't know why it was different, being on a stage and dancing compared to speaking. I had just the right amount of nerves before I got up to dance my parts. Those were only natural. But I didn't have to say a thing.

My body expressed everything that I needed to say. Speaking was entirely different, and those pre-stage nerves had nothing on this.

By the time Cassidy was ready for me, I was full-on shaking. "God, I need to get it together."

"Hey, hey," Isaac said. "Just look at me."

I looked deep into his eyes, and in that moment, I felt grounded. I could do anything. I didn't have to give this speech to everyone. I could just give it to him.

"You're going to do great," he told me.

"Thanks," I whispered and then broke away to stand before the crowd.

My palms were sweating, and my heart was already ratcheting back up, but every time I felt out of control, I brought my gaze back to Isaac. It was a short speech. Really more of a thank-you than anything. Nothing more than what Kathy had said at the beginning of the night. But still, by the end of it, I was uncomfortable and damn glad it was over.

When everyone left the room, I collapsed into a chair. "This was not how I'd thought this night was going to go."

Isaac chuckled and sat down next to me. "No, me neither."

"What did you expect?" I asked him hopefully.

"Well, I wanted to ask you out."

"Oh!"

He shrugged. "Feels like maybe too much with everything else going on."

"I'm only here for a month, Isaac," I warned him.

"I know. And I know that should matter to me." He reached out and took my hand. "But it doesn't."

My heart thumped a whole new rhythm in my chest. This was one of hope. I'd wanted Isaac Donoghue for as long as I could remember. It felt too right when I was with him. Saying no now would be absurd. Even if there was only a month...at least we'd have a month.

"Okay, I'd like that."

10

PEYTON

𝒦athy had a healthy, bouncing baby girl named Lily.

And in her next breath, she named me the interim artistic director.

In my shock, the only answer I could find was yes.

Cassidy had spent all day on the phone, trying to find someone to take over. The interim AD, who had planned to come in January, couldn't be here earlier than Christmas. She was running her own *Nutcracker* until then. And every other person that Cassidy could get to take her call couldn't do it. Everything was too short of notice. What person in their right mind would come in as the artistic director the day before opening night?

Me.

I was that idiot.

Luckily, I had more than twenty years of experience with *The Nutcracker*, and I had played every role. Though I didn't know all the choreography for this *Nutcracker* since Kathy had clearly re-choreographed some of the roles to her company members' strengths, I could at least get us through the last day of run-throughs and a full-dress rehearsal. And I did.

Dress rehearsal wasn't a complete disaster. Though I was ready to strangle Katelyn Lawson by the end of it. She had taken every opportunity to insert herself where she didn't belong. If she did that tonight, during opening night, then I was going to personally kick her out of the pre-professional company. I really didn't know how Kathy had dealt with her. If anyone acted like that at the School of American Ballet, they would be sent home. No questions asked.

Luckily, I hadn't heard a peep from her as we got ready for curtain rise. Nick had, thankfully, agreed to speak to the crowd. I had no interest in public speaking again, and our executive director was charismatic as hell. Let him work his magic while I stayed backstage.

"All set, Peyton," Cassidy said with a head nod.

"Good. Drosselmeyer is in position?"

Cassidy listened into her headset. "Yes, we're ready. Ten minutes."

A whispered chorus of, "Ten minutes," rang out to the other dancers.

A smile came to my face. At least all of this felt familiar. I stepped into the backstage area, crowded with young dancers in long dresses and suits and a few lonely mice, chatting excitedly.

A hand tapped my tights. "Miss Peyton?"

I turned in surprise to find the tiniest little mouse of

them all. I knelt down before her. "What can I do for you, Aly?"

Her mouse head was off, and she had a furrow in her brow. "I don't think that I can do this."

I raised an eyebrow in surprise. "Why not? You've been wonderful in rehearsals."

"But this isn't rehearsal. This is the *show!*" she answered emphatically, as if that made a difference. "There are people out there, watching. What if it's not perfect?"

"Want to know a secret?"

Aly nodded.

"No one is perfect. Not even me."

"Yeah, but—"

"I messed up onstage once, and you know what I did?"

She shook her head.

"I went back out onstage, and I did it right the next time. The only way we get better is to keep trying...even if it's not perfect."

Aly sighed heavily with all the drama of a five-year-old. "But I don't want to mess up."

"Let me show you something." I stood and held my hand out, which she took easily. I stepped back through the door that led to the wings.

The professional company stood in clusters, stretching and practicing particularly difficult turns to warm up. They all grinned as I walked a small mouse through them. A few even waved at Aly and said her name reassuringly. Distraction was also a good method, and Aly was well loved among the company.

I stopped right at the corner of the curtain. I held my finger to my mouth, and Aly nodded solemnly. Then, I pulled the curtain aside, barely an inch, so that we could both see out to the awaiting crowd.

And it *was* packed. My heart lurched with excitement and a flutter of nerves. Even the greatest dancers in the world got pre-show jitters. Which was why I didn't blame Aly at all. This was her first real show. I couldn't even remember mine, but I was sure that I'd been nervous.

"When I was a little girl, almost as young as you, I had stage fright, too."

Aly's eyes widened. "You?"

I put my finger to my mouth again and tried not to laugh. Her whisper hadn't quite been a whisper. "My favorite dance teacher told me, when I got nervous, I should look to this special place in the audience, and it would make me feel better."

"There's a special place to look?" she asked in awe.

I nodded and pointed. "You see that spot where you look up, right past the bottom level of seating, but not up to the balconies? It's a black spot, where they direct the music."

"I see it," she said in excitement.

"That's where you look, and *poof*, nerves go away." I let the curtain fall shut. "So, when you're onstage, if you get nervous, then you just find that spot, and everything will clear right up."

"Wow," Aly said with wide-eyed adoration. "Thank you, Miss Peyton."

Then, with a grin, she darted away. I could hear her giggling with her friends from here until a stage parent shushed them. I just laughed softly and went back to Cassidy.

"You're so good with her," Cassidy said.

I flushed and was glad she couldn't see it with the dark lighting and pound of makeup on my face. "There's always someone who's nervous before the first show."

"Well, I thought it was adorable. Isaac would be happy to know you're looking after his baby."

I blushed an even deeper, darker red.

"That's Nick's cue," Cassidy said after listening to her headset a moment.

I cleared my throat, putting the thought of Aly and Isaac out of my head. "Everyone, to your places. Quickly."

Then, the performance began in a flurry of rushing dancers preparing to take flight. The curtain rose, Drosselmeyer took stage in his workshop, and we were off. Cassidy handled the stage while I did final directions for the dancers until it was my time to perform the *pas de deux*.

I left all my troubles behind and soared into my role. Everything disappeared while I graced the stage, turning and leaping and floating before a full crowd. And when the audience went wild and the final curtain dropped, then, and only then...did I feel my knee.

A breath rushed out of me, and I leaned heavily into my right side. Everyone was so excited about how well opening night had gone that no one noticed me stumble back into the dressing room, where I washed down an ibuprofen with a giant bottle of water.

I had already changed into street clothes and had my

dance bag over my shoulder before the dressing room was flooded with the company.

Cassidy found me and drew me into a big hug. "That was incredible. I've never seen anyone dance that role like you."

"Oh, thank you, Cass. What do I need to do to help you clean up?"

She waved me away. "Go enjoy your night. I can take care of it."

"Oh no, are you sure?"

"People will want to congratulate you. It's opening night."

"All right. But if you need help tomorrow night..."

"I will let you know," she said with a laugh.

I ignored the pain in my knee and headed out the door to the lobby. This time, instead of being bombarded with overeager donors, I was bombarded with an even more eager group—my family.

A cheer went up at my entrance, and tears came to my eyes when I saw everyone I loved standing in one place. My mom and dad were there, holding a giant bouquet of flowers. Piper stood with her not-boyfriend, Bradley, and Peter was with his definite-boyfriend, Jeremy. Even my *abuelita*, Nina, had made it, looking as proud and strong as ever despite only being four foot nine.

When I had been young, we'd throw a party the year that each of us grew taller than Nina. We thought it was a great accomplishment to be taller than our grandmother. And she'd always reveled in the day, bestowing gifts on whoever had managed such a height and reminding everyone that she was still the smartest among us.

Abuelita came forward and wrapped me in a hug. "My Peyton, you looked wonderful out there tonight."

"*Gracias, abuelita.*"

"*Que es esto*? You cannot visit your grandmother now when you come home?"

I laughed and squeezed her tighter. "I have been busy, but I will be sure to visit."

My parents saved me by stepping forward and handing me the large bouquet. I hugged each of them as they lavished compliments on me.

Piper grabbed me next. "Even better than New York."

"No way," I said at once.

My family had come out almost every year to see me in a performance. They had seen too many *Nutcracker*s to count.

"Yes," Piper said. "You really lived in this one."

"Thank you," I said honestly.

"Nice work," Bradly said with a head nod.

"Yeah, it was okay," Peter said with a shrug.

I punched him in the arm. "Jerk."

He laughed. "Honestly, it would have been better if Jeremy hadn't spent the entire time discussing the merits of the ballet story to the actual children's literature."

Jeremy shrugged. "They bastardized the story."

I just laughed and shook my head as Jeremy launched into some explanation about lit theory that I had no chance of following.

Isaac wandered over then with his parents, Annie, and Aly, who was carrying a bouquet of flowers nearly as big as she was. My parents gave each of them hugs and offered praise to Aly, who bounced around with excitement for the completion of her first dance.

"I just wanted to say thank you," he said once we finally had a moment to talk.

"For what?"

"Aly told me that you helped her not to be nervous."

"Oh," I said, flushing.

"She had been nervous all day, and I didn't know how to fix it."

"Just...tricks of the trade. Nothing big."

"But it was," he said with that same perfect smile. "And I appreciate it. Are we still on for Wednesday?"

I bit my lip and nodded. "Can't wait."

Once my parents said hello to every person they knew in the entire lobby, we all finally retreated to the row of cars. I got into Piper's Jeep while she spent the next ten minutes chatting with Bradley and then leaving before he could kiss her. I didn't even have the energy to ask about that.

When we got home, I went straight for the freezer and filled an entire bag with ice.

Piper watched with wide eyes. "What are you doing?"

"Icing." I sank into the couch and expertly wrapped my knee with the ice packet.

"You said you were better."

"I am," I said through gritted teeth.

"Peyton!"

"It's preventative," I lied.

She dropped down next to me. "Why are you dancing if you're still hurt?"

"I'm not hurt."

She nudged my knee, and I yelped. "Peyton?"

"I'm fine," I said with a glare. "I am, like, ninety-five percent better, Pipes. Knees just take a long time to heal, and then they can give you trouble forever."

"Are you causing more damage by dancing?"

"No."

But if I were completely honest, I had no idea.

11

PEYTON

Blaire whistled at me as I stepped out of the back bedroom on Wednesday evening.

I'd rushed back from rehearsal and taken the fastest shower in existence. My hair, which always took nearly an hour to blow-dry, miraculously worked with me, and I managed to get it mostly dry in thirty minutes. I'd grabbed a pair of bootcut jeans and an oversize sweater. A wave of mascara and a dollop of lipstick later, and I had a whole three minutes to spare before Isaac picked me up.

"That's encouraging," I said with a laugh.

"Are you going on a date?"

I bit my lip and nodded. "Isaac asked me out."

Blaire's eyes widened. "This is so exciting! His first date since his wife died."

I nearly choked on those words and sank into the seat opposite her. "What?"

"Oh God, did I just ruin it?" She tugged her baseball hat over her eyes. "Forget I ever said that."

"Well, now, I can't." I jerked the hat off of her head. "He hasn't dated since Abby died?"

She slowly shook her head. "No. The guys tried to set him up on blind dates and shit, but he wasn't interested. He always says that Aly is his whole life."

"Why...is he going out with me then?"

Blaire shrugged once but grinned. "You must be special."

There was a pulse in my chest of excitement at that thought but also...fear. Maybe I shouldn't have ever agreed to this. If this was his first date in five years, then there would be expectations...right?

Before I could second-guess it, a knock came from the door. When I answered it, I found Isaac standing in the doorway, holding a bouquet of flowers.

"Oh my goodness," I whispered. "Those are for me?"

"No, I brought them for Blaire," he deadpanned

Blaire hopped up. "I'll take them!"

I laughed, taking the flowers out of his hand and bringing them to my nose. "They're beautiful."

Blaire winked at us. "I'll put them in a vase. You two go have fun."

"Thanks, Blaire," I said, passing her the flowers.

"Shall we?" Isaac asked.

I nodded and followed him out to his truck. It didn't hit me until I sank into the passenger seat that this was really happening. I was going on a date with Isaac Donoghue. The first one we'd been on since we were seventeen years old. It was surreal that I still had the same butterflies rattling around my stomach that I'd had when we first did this.

I tucked my legs into a pretzel and then reached for the radio dial, turning it up so I could hear the '80s rock song coming in through the speakers.

"Two minutes in my car, and you've already taken over the radio."

"You're not new here," I told him with a laugh as I started singing along to "Bohemian Rhapsody." "Plus, isn't this your favorite song?"

"Don't bring logic into this," he said, sliding his eyes to mine with a smile.

My stomach lurched. I wished I knew what magic he unfurled in my presence to make me such a young dope all over again. But in that moment, I didn't mind. It was nice to just be for once. Not have to worry about dance or anything else. Just me and Isaac.

"So, where are you taking me?"

"It's a surprise."

"Fine," I grumbled, flipping the heat up.

"Are you cold? Shouldn't you be used to it after living in New York?"

"For your information, I've never gotten used to the cold. Even in New York, it still chills me to the bone. And anyway, Lubbock has that weird weather thing."

He laughed. "What weird weather thing?"

"You know, where it's bright and sunny and seventy-five in the morning, and by the night, it's freezing and snowing and eleven degrees. It happens every year."

"But it's still fifty here. I don't think that's happened yet."

"Yet! But it will."

He just shook his head at me.

"What's Aly doing tonight?" I asked curiously.

"She's with Annie," he told me, veering the truck deeper south. I had a sense of where we were going, but I wasn't sure. "Annie just passed her last exams for the semester, so she's off until January."

"That's great. I'm sure Aly likes to spend time with her aunt."

"She does. She practically pushed me out of the house." He shook his head. "She's going to be a handful when she's older."

"Oh, but she's so great."

He beamed. "She is."

As we traversed the ever-increasing country roads, I finally turned and raised an eyebrow. "Are we going where I think we're going?"

He shrugged. "Where do you think we're going?"

"Sinclair Cellars."

He shot me a conspiratorial look and turned left down the road toward my family's vineyard and winery. I was confused, but I tried not to let it show. I hadn't really considered what we were going to do. Anything with Isaac was always its own form of magic. It had always been like that. But I hadn't anticipated our first date in sixteen years to be under the watchful eye of my family. I knew for certain that my dad and Piper were working tonight.

But as we came to a crawl before the main building used for wine tastings and dinner, my eyes lit up.

"Is that..." I whispered.

My jaw dropped. The vineyard was awash in Christmas lights. Every color imaginable lined row after row of grape vines. They seemingly went on forever. A light display that even outdid my father's amazing work on his home.

No one had told me that they were doing this. I'd had no clue. And I had no idea how it hadn't come up.

"Surprise," Isaac said with a grin.

"How is this possible?"

"It was supposed to be a coming-home surprise for you. Your dad has been working on it for over a month. When Piper found out we were going out, she said I should take you here. I think they were planning to show it off to you, but she graciously let me do it."

"This is amazing," I gushed. "I can't believe they were able to keep it a secret."

"It is rather unlike them," he agreed.

He parked out front of the mostly empty building, which was as large as a warehouse with a church-like facade. I'd never understood the significance of styling it as such, but people oohed and aahed over the terra-cotta roof and high-vaulted ceiling.

I jumped down out of the truck and turned my attention to the fields beyond the winery. I couldn't believe that they had done all of this for my return. Maybe my family had missed me being gone more than I'd realized.

Isaac gestured for us to head toward the building, but once we were close, we veered left toward a small booth with three large stainless steel thermos dispensers and a heater. Two college–aged kids sat behind the booth, holding hands and staying warm with the portable outdoor heater.

They jumped apart at our approach.

"Hi!" a wide-eyed girl said, her curly hair barely contained in her beanie. "Welcome to Sinclair Cellars. We have mulled wine, spiked hot chocolate, and cider."

"Two mulled wines," Isaac said, handing over his credit card and two paper tickets.

The guy, who was in a leather jacket and looked like he thought he was the coolest guy in existence, tapped the card on their machine and then handed it back with the two drinks.

"Enjoy the lights!" the girl said, already nuzzling back into her boyfriend as Isaac diverted us from the booth.

I held the beverage between my hands, grateful for its warmth. "They sure bring back memories."

"How many times did your dad corral us into working the hay rides in the fall?"

I groaned. "Too many to count. Though Piper still complains that I never helped out enough because of dance."

"I do remember lots of dancing, but I also remember sneaking off into the vineyards and making out."

"Oh my God," I said, covering my face, "I forgot all about that."

"How could you forget? We used to sneak out every shift."

"I know. I remember now. I just haven't thought of that in so long."

"We'd shirk half of our shift."

"The real reason Piper would get mad that I wasn't helping enough."

Isaac shrugged. "Worth it."

And it had been. Now that all the memories were

flooding back to me, I couldn't stop thinking about us out here every fall, helping my dad with the hay rides and then creeping off into the vines to escape the crowds. The feel of Isaac's fingers on my bare skin, tangled in my long hair, running down my back. The taste of him against my lips. The inability to think of anything but him in his presence. It had been a long time since I'd had that primal reaction to anything other than dance. It was a part of me, but Isaac intrinsically was, too.

My face heated at my wandering thoughts, and I was glad for the dark evening and the bright Christmas lights to hide behind.

"Oh, I almost forgot," he said, taking out his phone. "Piper said if I dialed into the radio station on my phone, it would play music the whole way."

He fiddled with the app that he'd downloaded ahead of time, and sure enough, "Frosty the Snowman" began to play. He shoved it into his back pocket. The music was a little muffled but not by much.

"So, what's it like, being the artistic director?" he asked as we took the first turn, following the directions to navigate the lights.

"Magical," I said softly. "But also difficult."

"Difficult because it's new?"

"Yes, and no. I've choreographed before and run rehearsals. It's part of being a dancer. Most professionals have some experience with it. But this feels like more than that. This is being in charge of the entire artistic direction of a company. It's a lot of pressure. *The Nutcracker* is the biggest event of the season."

"But you know every role. You've done this a thousand times."

"You're right. That part makes it easier. And it is wonderful. I love working with the company, especially the younger students." I took a long, soothing sip of my wine. "If I'm honest, I always thought I would become a director like this once my dance career was over. This just feels earlier than normal."

"Really? I thought you'd want to perform forever."

"I do," I said immediately. "More than anything."

I didn't bring up my injury. Or the pain that still radiated through my knee when I danced. I knew I couldn't dance forever, but I couldn't imagine giving it up either.

"But eventually, I mean, sometime in the future, I want to do this. It feels a bit like a test run."

"That's good though, right? You get to try out the job you think you want. Then, in, like, ten years, you can decide if you want to retire from ballet."

I laughed. Ten years. Very few dancers continued into their forties. I'd need a miracle to be one of them. But I didn't say that either.

"And you're working at Wright Construction," I said, changing the subject. "Tell me about that."

"Well, I'm the full-time project manager. I mainly oversee the largest projects we have, such as the Buddy Holly Hall."

"You helped build the performing arts center?" I asked in awe.

"Not build exactly, but I manage the teams. I'm in charge of organizing everything, making sure the money is coming in from all the right places. That sort of thing. I'm not really the boots-on-the-ground guy anymore. Actually, I'm pretty excited about a new project, but it's kind of a secret."

He looked at me with those bright green eyes, which asked me if I could keep a secret. And I shifted closer, wanting nothing more than to dive deep into that gaze and never surface.

"Yes?"

"Lubbock is getting a professional soccer team. It's Division II, but they've hired Wright to design and build it."

My eyebrows rose. "Wow! That's great news for you! And you get to be a part of it?"

"Yep. Jensen and Morgan brought me in to consult on the facility since I have experience."

"You must be thrilled."

He couldn't even come close to keeping the smile off of his face. "I am. I can't wait to get started and to have games to go to. I miss it so much." He took my hand, interlacing our fingers together. "Speaking of Wright, they're actually having a Christmas party next week. Do you have any interest in going?"

"With you?" I asked in surprise.

He laughed. "Yes, with me."

"I don't have anything to wear." Damn Piper for being right that I was going to need more than a carry-on's worth of clothes.

"You could wear this," he said with a shrug. "I don't care."

"A girl does not wear this to a Wright Christmas

party," I said with an eye roll. "I'll find something. I'd love to go."

We came to a corner of the lights that was the divider point. A few benches had been placed in a semicircle around the opening in the vines. The last couple had just vacated the area, leaving us all alone.

I finished off my wine, tossing the cup into a nearby trash can, and took a seat on the bench. Isaac dropped down next to me, and when he noticed me shivering, he wrapped his arm around my shoulders.

"I missed you, Peyton," he said softly.

I turned and met his gaze, suddenly realizing we were mere inches apart. My heart hammered in my chest. My mouth went dry. I was lost. Utterly and completely lost. How had so much time passed, and yet I felt exactly how I had all those years earlier? Isaac Donoghue completed me. And I hadn't known how empty I'd been living without him.

"Isaac," I whispered back.

His free hand came up and cupped my jawline, gently rubbing his thumb across my cheek. "Don't think about tomorrow. Just be here with me."

I didn't know how he had seen the fear in my eyes. The fear that I was leaving and this was going to break us even worse than the last time. But he saw, and it dissolved with his words.

He drew me in closer. Our noses touched in the dark. My breath hitched as the contact sent fire through my body, straight to my core. One little touch, and we sizzled. Anything more, and we'd cause an inferno.

"Isaac," I pleaded. Not knowing whether I was pushing him away or pulling him closer.

He didn't wait. He fit his mouth to mine perfectly. I groaned deep in the back of my throat as energy rushed through me.

Sixteen years I'd kissed these lips with tears running down my cheeks and salt on our tongues. Now, that was gone, and in its place was a sense of newness, of rediscovery.

Not hesitant, not questioning, but inviting and explorative. A heat suffused me, not from the wine, but from his lips and tongue and body. The way he eased away every tension I'd ever had. And I was completely subsumed by him. Not a single part of me wanted to walk away from this.

For I knew this boy—body, mind, and soul—and he'd stolen my heart long ago. This kiss sealed that he wasn't giving it back.

12

ISAAC

*P*eyton made me want to be reckless.

I knew Annie was at home with Aly. That I needed to get back. That I absolutely could not stay out all night with Peyton Medina. But God, a part of me wished that I were young and foolish enough again to do it.

We had finished our walk through the gardens and eaten off of a charcuterie board inside the tasting room. Peyton had another drink, but I opted out since I still had to drive. She had been giggly and tipsy from the alcohol. I just wanted to kiss those wine-stained lips all night. Being an adult sucked.

"Let's do this again," Peyton said as we stood on Piper's front porch. She leaned back against the wall. The alcohol had primarily run its course, but her smile hadn't lessened any. "I had a really great time."

"I'm glad," I told her. "I'd like to spend more time with you."

"When are you free?"

Ah, the kicker. I wasn't free. Between work and Aly, I was never free. And I hated asking my parents or Annie to watch Aly all the time. It didn't seem fair even though they claimed not to mind.

Peyton must have seen it on my face. "Or we could wait for the Wright party, if that's easier."

"I just have to work out babysitters."

"Right. No, that makes perfect sense."

"Peyton," I said, taking her hand again and drawing her into me.

She wrapped her arms around my neck, and her body was nearly flush against mine. My dick jerked in my pants, wanting her, always wanting her. If I could shirk my responsibilities, take her inside, and fuck her all night, I would. With her body against mine so invitingly, I really, really wanted to. But I couldn't. And after sixteen years, I could wait until I had a night to really enjoy her.

I brought our lips together one more time, pressing her back into the brick wall. She moaned softly against me. My hands moved to the hem of her sweater. Her breathing hitched at the touch of my hands on her bare skin. God, I was getting away with myself...and I couldn't seem to stop.

This was Peyton. I didn't want to stop.

Finally, she broke away with a strained laugh. "Do you...want to come in?"

Fuck. I really did.

But I reluctantly shook my head. "I can't." I stepped back, running a hand through my auburn hair. "I wish I could, Pey. But I have to get back."

She nodded, stood on her tiptoes, and softly kissed

me once more. "That's okay. You should get home. It's no big deal."

I had to clench my hands into fists to keep from grabbing her again. Fuck, I'd missed her.

"Good night," she whispered.

"Good night," I said, reaching for her hand one more time and pressing my lips to it.

She flushed at the contact and then disappeared inside.

I waited until the door closed behind her before heading back to my truck. The night was buzzing in my veins. My steps were light, as if I were walking on clouds. A part of me considered doing a silly romcom twirl right there in the driveway. As soon as I plopped down in the driver's seat, I realized what this emotion was flooding my senses—giddiness.

I hadn't felt like this in a long, *long* time.

When I made it back home, Annie was in the living room, watching Netflix. "Have a good night?"

"Yes. It was great. Thank you for watching Aly."

"Anytime. You know I don't mind. I love spending time with her."

"Well, I appreciate it nonetheless."

"You could have stayed out later, you know," she said, suggestively raising and lowering her eyebrows.

I laughed and went into the kitchen. I pulled two beers out of the fridge and handed one to Annie as I sank into the seat next to her.

"So...what happened?" she pried, taking a swig of her beer.

"Really, nothing much. We just walked around the vineyard and talked."

"And kissed?"

"And kissed," I confirmed.

And what a kiss it had been. Never in a million years had I thought that I'd get another chance with Peyton. She had been the girl of my dreams in high school, and she still was now that we were both adults. I'd just always thought that she was so far out of reach. What could a famous ballerina want with someone like me?

But none of that seemed to matter when I was around her. She was effervescent, and it just spilled into my life.

Annie did a little dance on the couch. "It is so good to see you happy again."

I shrugged and turned back to the TV. This wasn't a conversation I really wanted to have. "I've been happy."

"Bro..."

"Aly makes me happy."

"Well, obviously. How could she not? She's wonderful. But there are other kinds of happiness, and you know it."

"Yeah," I muttered.

"And Peyton has always brought that out in you. Look at you. You're all smiley."

I rolled my eyes at her. "I smile all the time."

She poked me in my side. "You know what I mean."

"All right," I said, warding her off. "I do know what you mean. And Peyton does make me happy and smile. I asked her to go to the Wright Christmas party with me."

Annie shrieked with excitement.

"Shh!" I hissed.

We both fell silent and listened to the back bedrooms in anticipation. Aly was a light sleeper on a good night. She had never really been a great sleeper. I remembered the early years when she wouldn't sleep anywhere but in my bed. It was still hard to get her to fall asleep in her own room. We'd been working on it a lot.

I breathed out in relief. "I don't think we woke her."

"Sorry. I got carried away. I'm just excited for you."

"I think I realized that when you insisted I go on this date tonight and all but pushed me out the door."

"Sometimes, you need the kick in the ass to get going."

I drained the rest of my beer. "Suuure."

"What? You do. Remember that time—"

But she didn't get to finish her sentence because we both heard shuffling down the hallway.

"Daddy," a small voice called.

Annie and I both groaned softly. She had woken Aly up. Shit.

"I can do it," Annie said.

But I was already on my feet, waving her off. "Aly Cat, I'm here."

Aly was standing in the hallway with her eyes half-closed. She yawned wide and then blinked when she saw me. "Daddy, I heard voices."

"It's okay. It was just me and Aunt Annie in the living room."

"Oh. Okay. Would you tuck me in?"

"Of course."

I picked her up and carried her back into her room. The space was decorated with moons and stars. They glowed brightly despite the late hour. I deposited her into her bed and tucked the moon covers up to her chin.

"There you are." I stroked her hair back from her face. "Did you have a fun time with Aunt Annie tonight?"

"Yes," she said with another big yawn. "I had mac and cheese for dinner, and she let me have ice cream."

I laughed. "That sounds like you were spoiled."

She gave me a sleepy grin that made me melt. "I missed you tonight."

My heart constricted. This girl. This beautiful, magnificent girl. My whole world. God, I loved her.

"I missed you, too, sweetheart." I kissed the top of her head. "Now, go back to sleep. I'll be here in the morning. Maybe we can have waffles before I go to work."

"Promise?" she breathed.

"Promise."

I kissed her again and then snuck out of the room, carefully closing the door behind me.

Annie grimaced when she saw me. "Sorry again."

I shrugged and went into the kitchen for another beer. "It's fine. She wasn't really awake. If she had been, she would have fought me to sleep in my bed, but she went right back to sleep."

"Well, that's good at least." Annie got to her feet and stretched. "I'm glad you had a good night, and I'm glad it's Peyton. I've always loved her. So do Mom and Dad."

"Yeah," I said, remembering the first time I'd brought Peyton home. She'd cast a spell on my whole family. A spell that she had cast on me, too. "When I'm with her, it feels like the entire world stops."

"I love that," she said, giving me a hug and heading out.

I stayed up later than I should have, knowing Aly would be up at the crack of dawn, requesting waffles. But I couldn't stop thinking about the date. I'd never been able to get Peyton out of my system. And tonight, I could still feel her working through me. I couldn't wait until I could see her again. Especially for a night when I didn't have to rush home.

Fuck, those thoughts wouldn't leave me alone either. I carried them with me into the shower as my hand remembered all the ways I'd intimately known her body. And I fell back into bed, sated but not satisfied, wanting Peyton even more than before.

13

PEYTON

"Yes, Bebe! That was excellent," I said in rehearsal. "Grab some water, and then we'll run through the whole thing one more time."

The Nutcracker had gone off without a hitch the weekend after my date with Isaac. After our opening-weekend success, the seats in the new Buddy Holly Hall were completely sold out. People were driving in from all over Texas to come see our production.

And in true Peyton fashion, I was trying to up the ante for the next round of performances this weekend. Which meant a lot of time in the studio and pushing all of the dancers to try to reach their potential.

Katelyn hurried back out into the studio space first. "Don't you think the understudies should go through it once, too?"

"You and Jake have been practicing it behind the leads the entire time."

"But it's not the same."

"If you want more time to do it, then you can stay after class to practice."

Katelyn pursed her lips. "That's not fair. I can do those moves just as good as Bebe."

The class gasped softly and then went deathly silent. Katelyn hadn't been subtle about her dislike that someone else was taking the spotlight from her. I suspected it had something to do with her feeling like she was *owed* her spot in the show. But I would brook no disrespect in my studio space.

"You might or might not be able to dance the *pas de deux* as well as Bebe. However, you were not cast as Clara. So, the statement is not only irrelevant," I said, standing statuesque and staring at Katelyn with all the strength my own instructors had instilled in me all these years, "but also rude and disrespectful."

"I wasn't being rude. I was just telling the truth."

"I don't care for your truth. Life isn't fair, Katelyn. If you don't like it, then you can get out of my classroom," I said, gesturing to the door.

Katelyn huffed and then stormed from the room.

Good riddance.

She'd cool off, and then maybe we'd actually get something done without her crowding Bebe all the time. The rest of the students gaped after Katelyn's sudden departure.

I clapped my hands to draw their attention. "Again, from the top."

By the time rehearsal was over, I felt beat. Katelyn hadn't returned, and her shiny white BMW was already gone from the parking lot. If she wanted someone to hold her hand and pet her hair, then she'd just be disappointed because I was the wrong person for that. Kathy sure knew I wasn't a hand-holder. Not for the first or the last time, I wondered if she had chosen correctly.

I headed home in my dad's company car and showered off the rehearsal. Then, I changed into something more comfortable and headed over to my *abuelita*'s home. She had been living in the same one-story house since the '70s when she had immigrated to America with my mom. It wasn't much, but children and grandchildren had been raised there and the house was completely full of love.

She had a garden out back, full of herbs and spices that she grew herself. She'd always told us, growing up, that we preserved our heritage in our food. Then, she'd pinch my cheek and say, "In our dancing, too."

Abuelita Nina had always been a strong advocate for me pursuing dance even if it wasn't the Mexican dances she had taught me as a girl.

"What is that smell?" I groaned as I entered the house.

Piper stuck her head out of the kitchen. "Only my favorite food in the world."

"Pozole," I said, just shy of drooling at the thought.

"There she is," my *abuelita* said, leaving the kitchen to give me a hug. "You finally made time for me."

"*Lo siento.*" I pulled back to give her a kiss on the cheek. "Dance keeps me busy."

"You find more time for me, *mi amorcita.*" *Abuelita* patted my hand. "Come and eat. The pozole is ready."

"All the fruits and none of the labor," Peter muttered.

I laughed and took a seat at the small wooden table, which had been there since my childhood and showed it all through dents and scratches along the top. My mom doled out bowls of the traditional Mexican fare. It was the same recipe that my grandmother had brought straight from Mexico and that her mother and her mother before her had been making back home. We ate the meal in near silence as we all devoured the succulent pork shoulder mixed with white hominy, decadent spices, and piping hot chilis.

My mouth watered, as I drained the entire bowl. "Back in New York, there are some pretty amazing traditional Mexican restaurants," I told the table. "But none hold a candle to this."

"Come home, and I will make it for you all the time," *Abuelita* assured me.

"As much as I'd like to stuff myself until I can't walk tomorrow," Piper said, "we have to go look for a date dress for Peyton."

I buried my face in my bowl.

"Are you going on another date with Isaac?" my mom asked.

"Why isn't he over here for my pozole?" *Abuelita* asked, busying herself with cleaning up the dishes. "He loves my cooking. Good boy always ate two helpings."

I looked up from my bowl with a sigh. "We are going to the Wright Christmas party. It's not a big deal."

"It's a big deal," Peter said with a laugh.

Piper shot him a look, and they hit knuckles. "It so is."

"This is why I don't tell you anything."

"It's nothing to be ashamed of," my mom said. "We're all happy for you. We want to see you settled down and married."

"With some babies," Nina added. "I need some great-grandbabies, you know?"

I shook my head in dismay. "Not this again."

"I guess that's our cue," Piper said, coming to her feet.

"Thank you for the dinner," I said, kissing my grandma as I passed and then my mom. "I will see you all after the show Friday, right?"

"We wouldn't miss it," my mom said with a wink. "Have fun."

I ignored her singsong tone and followed Piper out to the cars. We decided to leave the one I was borrowing from dad and take Piper's Jeep to her favorite boutique, Chrome.

We were greeted by an overexcited twenty-something with incredible style. "Hi, welcome to Chrome. Are you shopping for anything special today?"

"No, thanks. We're just browsing," I said automatically.

Piper rolled her eyes and grabbed my arm. "Actually, my sister is going on a date and needs a killer dress."

"Pipes," I muttered.

"Oh, that sounds fun. Where are you going?"

"The Wright Christmas party," Piper informed her.

"So, something cocktail. Not too sexy, but not too formal."

"It's really...I'm fine," I told them both.

"No worries. I'm Veronica. You go ahead and browse. I'm going to look for a few pieces on my own, and then we can consult in the dressing room."

I nodded gratefully to Veronica and began to wander the boutique. Piper followed behind me, adding things to my already-weighed-down arms.

"So, you and Isaac?" Piper asked, holding up a slinky red dress.

"What about us?"

"What's it like, doing this all over again?"

"I don't know," I said truthfully. But Piper looked honestly curious, so I continued, "It feels right. Not like it was in high school, but like it is meant to be now. It sounds so strange. I've dated other people. He was obviously married. This isn't like first love. It's different."

"Well, that was eloquent," Piper said.

I chuckled and snatched a miniskirt out of her hand, replacing it on the rack. "I wish I could describe it. When we were young and stupid, all I wanted was to marry Isaac Donoghue and live happily ever after. I gave that up for ballet."

"And now...what?" Piper asked.

I shook my head. "It feels like I'm reliving that fantasy. We're just taking this one day at a time."

"Far as I can tell, Pey, you and Isaac don't take anything one day at a time. There is an on switch and an off switch. That's it."

There was no way to refute that. It was true and always had been.

"I keep thinking that we're rushing into this, but when I try to stop it, I just can't."

Piper threw her arm around me as we headed back for the dressing room. "Well then, let's find the best outfit for the party. He's not going to be able to keep his hands off of you."

That was what I was hoping for.

14

PEYTON

*W*e found *the* dress.

Actually, Veronica found *the* dress.

It was something that I never would have tried on in a million years. A magenta silk that flowed to my ankles with a slit up one side and a plunging yet tasteful neckline. There was a tie at the back to hold up the straps since it plunged in the back, too. It hugged the figure I'd carefully cultivated in ballet, but it didn't make me look like I had no figure at all, which was the hardest part about shopping.

It was also more than I would have spent, but I'd decided to splurge and get the sparkly heels with ankle straps to go with it. Why not?

Blaire worked some magic with my curls, and I had no idea how it was possible. Half of me felt compelled to carry her around in my pocket at all times. I didn't really understand how a girl like her could do hair like this. She wore a baseball cap ninety-nine percent of the time and was always in an oversize T-shirt and leggings. No one would guess how fit she was under all those clothes either.

After borrowing a pair of Piper's dangly earrings, I was out the door. Isaac had wanted to come pick me up, but since his mom volunteered with United Way on Thursdays, and she was watching Aly, he wouldn't have been able to come get me on time. We would have been late to the party. So I'd just offered to meet him at his house.

When I pulled up to the sidewalk, his mom had just parked in the driveway.

"I'm here. I'm here," she said, hustling up to the front door. "I'm sorry. I got here as soon as I could."

"Grandma!" Aly cried and ran down the front steps.

"It's fine, Mom," Isaac said. "We're just glad you're here."

"I'm happy to see this little peanut," she said, pulling Aly into a hug. "Did you have dinner already?"

"Nope. I was thinking mac and cheese."

"Were you?" His mom looked up at Isaac, and they both laughed. Apparently, that must have been a common occurrence.

I'd been hovering with the car door open, trying not to butt into their conversation, but with a deep breath, I stepped out of the car. I reached for my jacket, feeling the chill seep into my skin. "Hello, Mrs. Donoghue."

"Miss Peyton!" Aly cried. "You look beautiful."

I laughed as I pulled my coat on. "Thank you, Aly."

"Hello, Peyton dear. Please just call me Marie." She pulled me into a hug. "And you do look beautiful."

"Thank you. And thank you for watching Aly."

"We're going to have so much fun," Aly said. "I have a gingerbread house we can make, Grandma."

"Do you? Well, why don't we go inside and put that together after we get some dinner in you? How does that sound?"

"Yes!"

"Give your dad a hug and kiss good-bye."

Aly darted back over to Isaac, who, up until that point, hadn't said a word. He was just staring at me in awe. I flushed at that look, which was both mesmerizing and filled with desire. But when Aly reached him, he broke his stare and lifted her into his arms, planting a kiss on both cheeks.

"Be a good girl for Grandma."

"Okay. I love you, Daddy."

He squeezed her one more time and then set her down. His mom kissed him on the cheek. "Have a good night," she said before taking Aly's hand and heading inside.

"You look stunning, Peyton. That dress..." He shook his head.

"Thanks. Piper helped me find something. I really didn't bring anything but dance clothes with me."

He took my hand and brought it to his lips. "It's perfect."

I flushed all over at the way he'd said it. The sultry quality to his voice and the heat layered through every syllable. It didn't hurt that he looked really fucking good. I'd seen him in a suit before, of course, after he got off work, but it had nothing on this one. It had clearly been tailored, and the sharp black material fit his broad shoulders and cut in sharply to his waist. I wanted to tug on his dark blue tie and pull him into me. The feeling was so intense that I actually took a step backward.

"The party," I managed to get out. As if saying it out loud might make it seem like something I was actually interested in...rather than finding a quiet place alone for the evening.

He chuckled softly and then walked around the truck to open the door for me. I thanked him and then settled into the passenger seat. The drive to the party was thankfully short. Truly, you could get anywhere in Lubbock in under twenty minutes, but the space was filled with lingering tension. I hadn't forgotten that kiss after our date...or how eagerly I'd invited him inside. We'd both known what that meant...what we wanted. And that heat hadn't cooled.

The Wright Construction Christmas party was being held at the Overton, a large hotel downtown, across from the Texas Tech campus. Apparently, it was usually held on the top floor of the Wright building, in their private restaurant, but some people had—correctly—requested someplace other than *work* for their big holiday event. The Wrights had complied.

We checked our coats at the door and then headed into the massive ballroom, decorated for the Christmas season in a collage of red, gold, and silver. Circular tables filled the perimeter of the room with gold-rimmed plates, festive red napkins, and extravagant floral centerpieces. Waiters in tuxedos walked the room, holding trays of bubbling champagne flutes. There were three open bars, which already had lines, and a stage at the back of the room with a band playing holiday hits. The room had three sets of doors, which opened onto a long marble balcony with an elaborately carved balustrade and outdoor heaters. Everything looked magical and flush with opulence.

Isaac stopped a passing waiter and grabbed us drinks. We drank a lot of champagne at ballet functions back in the city. It had taken me forever to get used to the taste, but now, I enjoyed it.

"I can't believe this," I said to Isaac with wide eyes. "They must have spent a fortune on this party."

"It's their biggest party every year. They host a number of charity events, but this is when they give back to the employees. Christmas bonuses went out today and then the party. Jensen always went overboard, but now that Morgan is the CEO, she's practically doubled the budget for it."

"*Morgan,* Morgan?" I asked in surprise. "Wasn't she a few grades younger than us?"

"Yeah. Two years, but she's really taken the mantle and owned it. No one wanted Jensen to step down, but Morgan is more than competent."

"Wow," I whispered.

CEO before she turned thirty. What an accomplishment.

"Come on. Let me introduce you to Jordan," he said, putting his arm around my waist. "He's the Wrights' cousin. He moved here from Vancouver, where he had been running the Canadian branch of Wright Construction. The minute he stepped in, he immediately took over the performing arts center. project At first, we were worried that he'd be pretentious, like he was entitled to the spot, but he might be the hardest-working person in the building. Well, since Jensen left at least."

"That's good. You don't want someone to come in who is lazy. We've had a few dancers come into the corps, but then they never go anywhere because they think they deserve their spots. It sucks."

"Yeah. Just like that. But I think you'll like Jordan. He's kind of a hard-ass, but he gets shit done, so I don't care."

"Jordan," Isaac said, firmly shaking his hand.

"Hey, Isaac. Good to see you, man."

"You too. This is my date, Peyton Medina."

I shook his hand, and he was no less aggressive with me. "Pleasure to meet you."

"The pleasure is all mine," he said with the signature Wright smile.

I'd gone to school with Landon Wright. I knew *exactly* what that smile was like. Even if I'd never had any interest in any of the Wrights, that didn't mean they weren't all fabulously attractive and charismatic. Jordan was no different with his short, dark European-styled hair and scorching brown eyes. His suit was a deep navy blue, and he wore it like he belonged in it.

"Isaac was just saying that you're the hardest worker at Wright Construction."

"Well, that's a compliment if I've ever heard one," Jordan said. "Isaac is the best man on my team. I wouldn't be half as accomplished without him at my side."

Isaac laughed. "Thanks, Jordan. Are you coming to the game on Sunday?"

"Oh, right," I said, putting two and two together.

"You're Julian's brother. He doesn't work for the company?"

"That's right," Jordan said. Something wavered in his eyes at the question. "No, Julian...isn't working for the company. Our mom was sick when we moved here and went through chemo. He took the time off to take care of her."

"Oh," I whispered in horror. "I'm so sorry."

"It's fine," Jordan said, waving it away.

"In other news," Isaac said quickly, "Julian *is* looking at opening up a winery with Hollin."

Jordan sighed. "It does look like that venture is in the works."

"Well, Peyton's family knows a thing or two about it. Julian should reach out."

"I don't know much, honestly," I said. "But I could get them in contact with my sister and my dad."

"Julian has always had pipe dreams," Jordan said with a shrug. "We'll see what actually comes of it."

"I can give you my phone number, if he wants to reach out to my dad. He's always happy to help others get started in the industry," I told him earnestly.

"Sure. Doesn't hurt," Jordan said.

We exchanged numbers, so I could get Julian in contact with the right people. It felt weird, being the one with connections in Lubbock when I didn't even live here anymore.

"So, the game?" Isaac asked.

Jordan glanced away once and then back. "Is Annie playing?"

"Yeah. She and Blaire are wiping out the competition," Isaac said, proud.

"I'll see if I can make it," Jordan said noncommittally.

But I had seen something else when Jordan asked the question. It wasn't the same thing Isaac had heard. Call it female intuition, but there was something going on there. I wondered what exactly was going on with Annie and Jordan Wright.

"Is Jordan giving you a hard time?" Jensen Wright asked, appearing at Isaac's side.

Isaac laughed. "I think I'm giving him a hard time actually."

"And who is this?" Jensen asked.

I swallowed and met his gaze. I might have been five years younger than Jensen, but I remembered thinking he was so hot when I was a kid. Couldn't deny it now either.

"My date, Peyton Medina."

"Medina," Jensen said as he shook my hand. "Any relation to Matthew Medina?"

"That's my dad."

"He's a great man. He owns Sinclair Cellars, right?"

I nodded.

"That has been a perfect venue for us for smaller events. Do you work there?"

"Oh, no. I'm a ballerina with the New York City Ballet."

Jensen's eyebrows rose. "Wow. That's incredible. I wonder if I've seen you perform before. I'm in Manhattan regularly."

"Perhaps," I said with a smile.

"Jensen Wright," a voice cried, stepping out of the crowd. A woman with a small pregnant belly approached him with fire in her dark eyes.

I was shocked to recognize her as Emery Robinson.

"Oh boy," Jensen muttered, unable to hide his grin.

"You're in so much trouble," Emery said.

"What did I do now?" Jensen asked.

She pointed to her belly. "Look what you did to me. This is all your fault."

My eyes rounded, but Jensen just shot me a wink. "Don't worry. She's always like this."

Emery seemed to notice me and stopped. "Oh my God, Peyton?"

"It's me."

"Whoa! You look exactly the same." She glared at Jensen. Though I saw the humor in her face now. "Instead, I look like a whale."

She did *not* look like a whale.

I pointed between them as Jensen wrapped his arm around Emery. My confusion must have registered. I clearly had not seen her since high school, but she definitely had been dating Landon Wright then.

"This is not the right brother," I said.

Emery laughed. "Uh...yeah, some things have changed since high school."

"As much as I would love to stay and hear the rest of this conversation," Jensen said, kissing Emery's hand, "I need to steal Jordan and Isaac for our announcement."

"Fine," Emery said. "But you owe me big later."

"Tacos," he purred.

"Don't act like you know me."

"Oh, but I do, baby," he said, nipping at her ear.

"And this is why I'm pregnant, ladies and gentlemen," she said as Jensen walked off with Isaac and Jordan.

"I don't think I'd be complaining."

We both giggled as the boys disappeared through the crowd.

15

ISAAC

"*P*eyton seems nice," Jordan said.

"We actually dated in high school. She's here for *The Nutcracker* season."

"Oh, wow." Jordan laughed and ran a hand back through his hair. "If I saw one of my high school girl-friends, I think I'd run."

I snorted. "Yeah, but you have girls falling at your feet."

"Nah, not *all* the time," Jordan said with a wink.

We laughed and came to a stop at the side of the stage, where Morgan was already waiting for us. Morgan was the most capable person I knew. Jensen was a brilliant mind. Jordan was a bulldozer. But Morgan...she ran everything. And she did it damn well.

"Oh good, you found them," Morgan said, looking up from her iPad. "Are we ready?"

Jensen crossed his arms over his chest and grinned at his sister. "Are *you* ready, Mor?"

She rolled her eyes. "Always."

"Should we wait for David?" Jordan asked after the CFO.

"I'm here," David said, jockeying for position in the circle.

"About time," Morgan said, skipping back through her notes. "I'll leave the iPad on the podium. Feel free to use it as much as you need. David is going to take the closing statement. Any questions?"

We all tried to keep a straight face. Morgan was the best, but she treated everyone with kid gloves regardless of the fact that both Jensen and Jordan had done her job before. It was just who she was.

Morgan stepped up to the podium first. She quieted the crowd and thanked everyone for coming. Then, she went into a speech about how well the year had been and how lucky the company was to have each and every person in attendance.

"Now, we want to make one more special announcement before all of you go back to your cocktails," Morgan said and then gestured for us to come onstage.

I followed behind Jensen and Jordan, feeling the momentous occasion. It didn't feel possible that I was here right now with three of the most important people at Wright. Three Wrights at that. But I'd been included, and no one seemed to blink that I was as valuable to the team.

"Thanks, Morgan," Jensen said, taking the mic. "We do have an exciting, new announcement. Thanks to Jordan's hard work and connections, we're officially bringing a professional soccer team to Lubbock."

The crowd cheered at this news.

He waited a minute before raising his hand. "That's right, and Wright Construction got the contract to begin building the stadium in the new year. I'm already working on the designs with the league. Jordan is going to be on point for the stadium, and Isaac is going to be the head project manager. I can't wait to see this come to fruition and see what else Wright has in store for us in the future."

The crowd applauded again and began to talk among themselves about the new soccer facility. It felt incredible to be privy to such information, to even be standing here as the announcement was made.

My smile stretched ear to ear as I stared out at my sea of colleagues. And then I found Peyton. She was clapping softly with her own wide smile. Her eyes glowed with pride. This wasn't what I'd planned when I graduated high school and went off to play soccer, but life had a way of guiding you onto a new path. This was mine. And somehow, it had put Peyton back on it.

We stepped offstage as David gave the closing remarks. I entered a sea of Wrights. Jensen and Morgan stood with the rest of their siblings—Austin, Landon, and Sutton. Their cousins, Jordan and Julian, had disappeared out of the main circle, and I moved to step aside but was drawn into the Wright circle.

"I see you brought Isaac in to do the real work," Landon said, shaking my hand.

He'd been the star quarterback when I knew him in high school, but he was a professional golfer now.

"Always here to make sure things get done," I told him.

Austin laughed and crossed his arms. "Do you ever get sick of making the same speech over and over?"

Morgan arched an eyebrow. "Do you ever get sick of the sound of your own voice?"

"I do!" Sutton said, raising her hand. "Austin's voice is obnoxious."

"Whose side are you on?" Austin grumbled.

Landon just chuckled into his drink. "Classic."

"Listen here," Morgan said, playfully pointing her finger at her brother. "If you think you can do better—"

"He can't," Landon butted in.

Sutton dissolved into giggles.

Jensen just sighed heavily and rolled his eyes. "Children, can we not?"

"Sure, *Dad*," Austin said, clapping his brother on the back.

Jensen shot Austin a perfect *dad* look, proving his point. "I've just had so much practice."

Then, his eyes wandered to his pregnant wife, who approached with Peyton.

I stepped away from the Wrights and their family antics. Some things would never change.

Peyton touched my hand, and her smile was still wide with pride. "You're so fancy. Up on a stage with the head of the company."

"Nah," I said, running a hand back through my hair. "It was nothing."

"Whatever. We both know that's not true. It was a big deal."

I beamed. "Yeah. It felt pretty good to get recognized

like that, and I can't wait to start working on the soccer complex."

"You've really found your place," she said.

"I never would have thought it'd be at something like this, but...yeah, I think I have." I took her hand in mine. "Let's go get another drink."

We waited in line at the bar, and I got a bourbon and Coke while she stuck to champagne. Then, we wandered out onto the mostly empty balcony. Peyton moved closer to a heater, and I offered her my jacket, which she let me slip around her shoulders. She pensively stared out over downtown Lubbock.

"What are you thinking about?" I asked her.

She frowned and then met my gaze. Her dark chocolate eyes were depthless, and I wanted to dive in and disappear. Fuck, I wanted more than that. I wanted her. I wanted her more than I ever had. Sixteen years had made me think that this could never happen. I'd moved on. I had a life. One that was taken away too fast, but I still lived. But then she had walked back into my presence, and suddenly, everything was upside down. We were only right side up when we were together. How had I survived all this time without her?

"I missed it here," she said softly.

"You sound...sad?"

"No, it's not that. It's just that this is such a different world. In New York, I feel like...I'm always swimming upstream. There's this endless current that I'm battling against. I don't exactly belong there even though I've lived there nearly as long as I lived here. But everyone is constantly hustling. And I liked that for a long time. I felt like it gave me that push to always be better." She shrugged one shoulder. "But here, I just...I don't know..."

"Fit?"

"Yes," she said, touching my arm. "Here, I just fit. No expectations. No constant struggle."

"You could come back," I said, the words slipping out before I could stop them.

I wanted to ask her to come back. I wanted her to be here. To be here with me. But I hadn't meant to ask her to do it.

She smiled softly but remained silent. I wasn't sure if I'd overstepped the bounds. This was all new. Even if we'd been here before, we weren't in the same place.

"Look, forget I said anything. Lubbock will always be your home, is what I meant..."

"No, it's okay," she said. She swallowed and met my gaze again. "Sometimes, I want to come home."

"You do?"

"Sometimes."

But not enough to do it. I knew better than to say that this time.

She laughed and clutched my jacket tighter around herself. "I'm sorry. I don't want to be sad tonight. This has been a great night. I'm glad that you invited me."

"You don't have to pretend with me, Peyton."

"I'm not pretending." She stepped forward and ran her hand down the front of my shirt. "And I just want to be with you tonight." Her voice dropped, low and sultry, as she looked up at me from beneath her lashes.

My hands slipped around her waist, pulling her in

closer. "Good. Though...I do understand the allure of New York."

She shook her head with a tilt of her head. "Have you ever been there?"

"I have," I said. I slid my hand up to cup her jaw and dropped my mouth until it was only an inch from her lips. "I came to see you."

"What?" she gasped, nearly touching my lips. Her eyes went wide. "When?"

"After I left the soccer team at SMU, I flew out to New York. I bought a ticket to your show and went to see you dance."

"I had no idea. Why didn't you say something?"

"I planned to. I bought flowers. I waited for you after the show. And then, when you came out, you were with your dance friends. You were laughing and looked so happy. I could see that it was the place for you. I wanted to say something, but I couldn't see a way for it to ever work. I couldn't move to New York, and you were never coming home."

"Isaac..."

"So, I dumped the flowers and came back. I knew that ballet was what you were made for, so we never had a chance. But now, you're here, Peyton, and you're the only thing I want."

I didn't wait for her response. I just pushed her body back against the balcony railing and brought my lips down onto hers. There was no hesitation. There was nothing soft or tender about the moment. I'd finally told her the secret I'd been harboring for years. I had never stopped thinking about her. I would have gone to the ends of the earth to be with her. But not at the expense of her happiness.

But now that we had a chance...there was nothing I wouldn't do to keep her in my arms.

She pulled back, breathless. Her eyes dilated in the faint light. Her fingers clutched my shirt.

"Do you...want to get out of here?" I asked.

"Yes," she said, a flush coming to her cheeks. "I thought you'd never ask."

16

PEYTON

saac Donoghue had come to New York for me.

My mind was still reeling. I'd thought about him and pined over him for years after he told me to leave to go to New York. It had been the right decision. But he was my first love, my first everything. I hadn't wanted to let him go, and my heart never left him behind.

It was different, knowing that he felt the same. That he'd wanted to make it work, but once again, he'd chosen my happiness over his. And now, we had this moment. I refused to waste it.

We exited the ballroom and grabbed my jacket from the coat check. I switched out jackets with him, pulling him on instead, as I headed toward the parking lot, but Isaac stopped me and held up a hotel key.

I raised my eyebrows. "Did you get a room?"

He shrugged. Not at all sheepish, like he would have once been. He took my hand and pulled me toward the elevators. "Thought we might have use for it."

"Cocky," I said as I crossed the threshold of the elevator.

His eyes gleamed as he walked me back against the opposite wall. "You were the one who invited me in last time."

"I was." I was breathless as he ran his hands up the silk of my dress. It was as if he burned his way up my body, dragging his fingers across the muscular contours of my back. My fingers threaded through his tie, just like I'd wanted to do earlier outside of his house, and I tugged him toward me. "Offer still stands."

"Good," he ground out as he finally fit his hips against mine.

His erection was evident, even through the layers of material, and a small gasp escaped my lips. He smirked as if he knew exactly what he was doing to me.

And God, how many times *had* we been here before? Desperate to strip our clothes off and fall into each other's arms. We'd learned the language of love from each other's bodies. Both of us were adults now, well versed in what the other wanted but with more experience than when we'd been fumbling teenage in uncontrolled hormones.

Isaac leaned in, his breath hot against my lips. "I'm going to take you up on that offer, if you don't mind."

I swallowed, my body a treacherous, wanton thing. "You'd better."

I'd forgotten. It sounded ridiculous, even in my own mind. But I'd forgotten what it was like to be desired. Not just for convenience or anything like that. But to be honestly and completely *wanted*. The look in Isaac's eyes said that he could hardly wait another minute before shredding this new dress to pieces and taking me right here in the elevator.

My body thrummed in response as our lips finally met. It had all the fervor that we'd been holding back. Knowing that we both had to be responsible adults and return to our commitments. But there were no responsibilities or commitments here. There was just two people who wanted nothing more than to forget the rest of their lives existed.

His hand snaked under the slit in my dress and hiked my leg up around his waist. I gasped again as he held me in place and ground against me. Our tongues moved together in rhythm with our bodies. I half-considered pushing the Stop button on the elevator.

The elevator dinged, and we hastily broke apart. My lips were swollen, and my lower half was pulsing in time with my desire. He grinned again and kissed me once more.

"This is how you should always look," Isaac said as we left the elevator.

I laughed. "How?"

"Unbridled."

He wasn't wrong. In dance, I was perfectly put-together Peyton. But for the first time in a very long time, I was letting my hair down.

Isaac located our room and tapped the card to give us access. My eyes swept the accommodations. A junior suite with a large waterfall shower, sitting area, and an oversize king-size bed at the center. The curtains were drawn to reveal a view of the lit city below us. But my eyes were only for Isaac.

"This is nice," I told him.

He crooked his finger at me. "Come here."

My heels carried me across the room. He still stood nearly a head taller than me, even in my heels, but I stood before him with my back straight and head held high.

"You don't need this anymore," he said, pushing my jacket off of my shoulders and tossing it to the chair behind him. His hands slipped down my arms and then back up my waist, leaving a trail of goose bumps in his wake.

I stepped forward into him. "Then, you don't need this."

I ran my hands under his suit jacket and helped him out of it. I dropped it next to mine then began deftly unbuttoning his shirt, one white button at a time. When I finally reached the bottom, I wrenched the shirt open, tugging it from its constraints and exposing the six-pack underneath. The sight of his body was so familiar and yet so new. I trailed my fingers over every ridge of his abdomen until I reached the seductive V that disappeared into his pants.

I hesitated only a moment before pulling his belt through the buckle. He inhaled sharply as I undid the belt and then popped the button open. My hands trembled slightly as I dragged the zipper to the base, caressing his dick through the material.

He jerked me forward almost involuntarily, and then his mouth was on mine. Needy and desperate. He'd been holding back, and I didn't realize how much we'd both been restraining ourselves until that moment.

Isaac buried his hands in my hair, and his tongue stroked mine before he dove downward, leaving a trail of kisses down my neck and across my collarbone. His hand found the scant string holding my dress up, and he tugged it loose. The straps tumbled off of my shoulders, baring me from the waist up.

He growled deep in the back of his throat at the sight of my breasts, nipples brown and erect. His mouth dipped down to taste them, as if he were seated before a feast and I was every course. My head fell backward as one hand palmed my breast and the other tweaked my peaked nipple.

My words were incoherent. A combination of, "Yes," and, "Please," and "Oh God," and I wasn't sure how much of it was in Spanish or English, but Isaac didn't seem to care.

I stepped backward as he led me to the bed and then laid me out on my back. Heated moans escaped my lips as his lips ran down my body, trailing kiss after kiss down my exposed stomach. He peeled the rest of the dress down my narrow hips and tossed the expensive material to the floor carelessly. Truth be told, I couldn't seem to care either.

All that was left between us was my nude thong. I whimpered as he teased the edges of the material with his fingers.

"Isaac," I pleaded.

But he didn't heed me, just left me to writhe on the bed as his tongue took over. He licked his way across the seam and down between my legs, spreading me wider before him. My breath hitched as he dipped one finger into my thong, feeling my slick wetness proclaiming my want for him.

"Peyton," he growled like a prayer.

Then, my thong was gone, and his mouth replaced the material. At the first touch of his lips on my core, I knew that I was a goner. Utterly and unequivocally.

He licked and sucked on my clit, building me to a crescendo like a virtuoso. And then his fingers began to play the melody, inserting one inside of me and then another. In and out while his tongue finished off the rhythm. Until I exploded on his mouth, letting him taste my desire.

While I was still lying helpless on the bed, he retrieved a condom from his back pocket and then shucked the rest of his clothes to the floor. He deftly fit the condom it to himself. My eyes widened at the sight of him. No wonder no one else had ever compared. He grinned when he caught me watching him. Then, he was prowling after me.

I crawled backward on the bed and watched how he was barely keeping himself from plunging into me.

"Peyton..." he began, prepared to ask my permission. As if I weren't already spread wide for him and begging him.

"Please," I gasped. "Please, Isaac. I want you...this."

That was enough for him. His strong body covered mine. Our hips fit together, as they had so many times before. His biceps flexed powerfully as he held himself up over my body. Our eyes met, locked. The world disappeared.

The head of his dick settled against me. My eyes rolled back in my head, and I lifted my hips to meet him. He chuckled at my attempts to get him to move.

"Needy," he growled.

"Aren't you?"

He pressed a firm kiss to my lips. "Always with you."

And then he eased into me. Inch by delicious inch until I was full to the brim. Everything went hazy with pleasure.

He dropped to his elbows, bringing our lips back together, whispering sweet nothings as he started up a rhythm. My body remembered the steps to this dance. Our bodies came apart and reconnected. I met him halfway until the slapping of our joining bodies was perfectly in sync.

As if Isaac had just remembered my flexibility, he pulled back and lifted my leg, hoisting it over his shoulder. My body contorted into a split, getting him deeper and deeper as he drove into me again and again. His eyes shuttered, and he lost all sense of control. I cried out as everything built within my body.

"Isaac," I cried. "I'm close."

"Come with me, love," he breathed against my skin.

The world exploded.

I dragged my nails down his back, leaving scratch marks as I fell into oblivion. My orgasm hit me like a two-by-four. Isaac roared his pleasure into the hotel room.

My legs shook as I came down from the high. Then, he collapsed next to me. Both our chests were heaving, and a fine layer of sweat coated our skin. Maybe we would make use of that shower after all.

I curled into Isaac's side. He slipped an arm around me and kissed the top of my head. This was even more familiar. This was perfect.

"I missed you," he breathed.

"Mmm," I mumbled.

He laughed. "No words?"

"I have words," I said, mischievously glancing up at him. "I hope you have another condom."

His eyes turned predatory once more, and he rolled me over on top of him. I straddled his hips.

"Round two already?"

"I don't think either of us should plan to sleep tonight," I said, teasing him with my hips.

He dug his fingers into my skin. "I hadn't planned on it."

Then, he brought our lips together, and I was lost to him all over again.

17

PEYTON

"Stay in bed a little longer," Isaac said, grabbing me around the middle and tugging me back down.

I giggled and nuzzled into him. "We're going to be late for work."

"Technically, I don't have to work today."

I huffed, "No fair."

"I'm going to go in anyway because I have a million things to do before we take a week off for Christmas. But maybe only a half-day."

"Half-day sounds better."

"What do you have to do?"

I peeked up at him. "I have some work to take care of for Kathy. No rehearsals today for me to cover. And then the show at seven."

"So...you might be free by the afternoon?"

"I might," I said with an arched eyebrow.

"Any interest in coming over later? Aly and I have plans to make Christmas cookies."

128

My heart lodged in my throat. He was asking me to hang out with him and his daughter. That was a huge step.

"Are you sure?" I whispered.

He placed a kiss on my forehead. "I'm sure."

"All right. I'd love to. Let me text you when I'm done with work, and then I'll come over."

"Good," he said, pulling me into another long kiss. "Because I can't imagine going another day without seeing you."

I flushed from head to toe. "Is that so?"

"It is. How do you feel about that?"

"Right now? Like I don't want to get out of this bed."

He laughed. "Fine. I'll be the responsible one. We should get to work. If we hurry up, then I'll see you sooner."

"That is good logic, Donoghue."

I hopped out of bed, and he smacked my ass as I reached for my discarded dress.

I yelped, "Watch it."

"How could I do anything else? Look at that ass."

I rolled my eyes and shimmied back into my dress. "Hours of ballet will do that."

"Won't find me complaining," he said as he pulled his suit back on.

He tugged me tight one more time and kissed me breathless before driving me back to Piper's house.

I tiptoed through the dark, empty house and just made it into my room when I heard a parade of feet running toward me.

"You didn't come home last night!" Piper cried.

I sighed heavily. "I didn't."

"And you're still in your dress."

"Yep."

"I'm so *proud* of you!" Piper said with a laugh. "Tell me everything. Well, not *everything*. Ew. But tell me most things."

"As much as I would love to do that, I really need to shower and get to work."

Piper pouted, sticking her bottom lip out. "Come on. At least tell me something."

I waved her off and headed toward the bathroom. "Isaac and I were together last night, and I'm seeing him again when I get off work."

"Eep! That sounds serious."

I paused before walking into the bathroom and contemplatively looked back at Piper. "It is, I guess."

Piper started to ramble about her excitement. I knew why she was so excited. She thought if I was happy enough with Isaac, as I once had been, then I might make a different choice. I might decide to stay here in Lubbock instead of go back to New York. But I didn't want to think about that choice. Or the fact that I really only had one more week in town.

My chest tightened. One more week. It wasn't enough time.

I shook my head to drown out Piper's ranting and grabbed a quick shower. Afterward, I pulled my hair up into a messy bun, threw on leggings and my favorite sweater, and then went straight back out the door.

The radio announced a storm on the horizon. Possibly the first snowflakes of the season. I'd believe it when I saw it. Lubbock weather tended to do whatever it wanted. Snow when it wasn't in the forecast and clear skies when it was supposed to snow. Everyone prepared like a blizzard was coming, but no one really believed it would happen.

When I parked in front of the studio, a couple in power suits was already waiting for me at the entrance. I took a deep breath before exiting. The wind buffeted against me as I jogged to the front door. Maybe a storm really was coming.

"Hi. Sorry I'm late," I said, reaching for my keys. It was only five minutes, but the look on their faces told me everything I needed to know about what was about to happen. "Can I help you?"

"Yes, I'm Angelica Lawson, and this is my husband, Bart."

"Ah, you're Katelyn's parents," I said, realizing immediately where this was going. I pushed the front door open and gestured them inside. "Why don't we go into the office, and we can talk?"

I directed them down to Kathy's office, dropping my purse on the floor next to the desk and taking an authoritative seat. Katelyn's parents settled uncomfortably before me. They were middle-aged and clearly well off, based on their appearances. Angelica's suit was top of the line, and her forehead didn't move. I recognized the signs from the donors back in New York. Bart's hair was thinning, and he wore a grim expression, as if it were his job.

"Now, how can I help you?" I asked, raising my chin and waiting for the inevitable.

"We came to discuss your mistreatment of Katelyn," Angelica said haughtily.

"Mistreatment?"

"You kicked her out of class!" Angelica cried.

"I did no such thing," I said immediately. "I told her that if she wouldn't comply with my rules that she could leave, and she chose to do so."

"You had no right," Bart growled.

I held my hand up. "Before you continue, I would like to make it quite clear that I have every right to run my classroom as I see fit. I am not here to coddle the children. I am here to teach them to be better dancers and ideally better humans in the process. My goal is for everyone to reach their potential through hard work and discipline. If you do not like that, then there is nothing more we have to say here. Katelyn is not required to take my classes. She *is* required to follow directions while she is there. If she doesn't like that, she can leave, which she did of her own volition."

"We didn't donate all of our time and hard-earned money to this company to have our daughter be treated like this," Angelica said, coming out of her seat.

"Treated how exactly?" I asked.

"Like she is beneath you," Bart raged. He stood, too.

Both of them towered over me, but I refused to rise to my feet, to give them the satisfaction of thinking I was flustered.

"She's not beneath me. This has nothing to do with me in fact. She is a student, and I am her teacher as well as the artistic director. She has to follow the rules, just like anyone else. No amount of time or money will change that."

"How dare you!" Angelica said. "Katelyn is the best dancer in the pre-professional company. She has already been accepted to Joffrey's summer intensive. How do you think it will look for her to leave your studio in her last year?"

"I don't know, Mrs. Lawson. My senior year, I'd already been admitted to the School of American Ballet in New York City." I smiled sweetly.

"That is beside the point," Bart said, flustered.

"Katelyn should have been cast in the role of Clara over that talentless hack who showed up two years ago," Angelica spat in her anger.

My heart hammered in my chest, but I carefully laid my hands out before me on the desk and slowly came to my feet. I wasn't taller than either of them, but I'd had years of dealing with entitled people who believed someone else should take my spot. I would not see the same happen to Bebe if I could help it.

"I would appreciate it if you did not resort to insults. Everyone who is in the pre-professional company is talented. That goes without saying. Bebe might have less experience, but she is the hardest-working student in the company, pre-professional or otherwise," I said flatly. "If you are going to continue to insult the institution that you believe you are defending, then you, like your daughter, can see yourself out."

"We're going to go to the board about this," Bart threatened.

"By all means," I said neutrally. Meanwhile, I was

holding back the scream threatening to break free from my lungs.

"We'll have your job," Angelica snarled as she rushed toward the door. "We're very powerful attorneys."

"That is great to know. I'd be happy to hear what the board has to say."

They each threw me one more glare before leaving my office. I collapsed back into my chair and groaned. My whole body was shaking with anger at the interaction. How dare they think that they could threaten me! How dare they come here and try to force my hand!

I took a few deep breaths and then jotted out a text to Kathy, letting her know what had happened. She responded instantly. Apparently, unsurprisingly, it wasn't the first time this had happened. She would talk to the president of the board and with Nick. I felt relieved that it wasn't on my shoulders, but I felt an even greater need to shield Bebe. Katelyn was out for blood.

I still held my phone, debating on whether or not to say something to Bebe at the show tonight when it vibrated in my hand. I looked down in surprise at the text message from Katherine Van Pelt.

I finally have a moment to myself. Coffee? Please tell me there's good coffee in this town!

Coffee. God, that sounded good. I stared at the pile of paperwork I needed to get through, but I just didn't have it in me after that fight with Katelyn's parents.

Monomyth on Broadway. See you in ten?

Monomyth was an all-white brick building just off of the Texas Tech campus on a bumpy red brick street. The word *coffee* was labeled in large red letters down the side of the building, and the inside was just as adorable with a cluster of tables usually filled with college students pretending to study. The best part was the incredible aroma whenever you stepped inside. Divine.

I ordered a latte and then took a seat by the window to look at the clouds rolling in on the horizon. Katherine appeared a minute later, looking gorgeous with her long, flowing brown hair and somehow so out of place. She belonged on runways and in boutiques on Fifth Avenue and strolling through Central Park. She hardly looked like the type to come to a quaint college coffee shop in Lubbock. But here she was, in pencil skinny jeans, a tucked-in white button-up, and a red peacoat that matched her lush red lips.

I waved at her, and she came to sit down after she had some kind of skinny iced mocha concoction in her hand.

"Iced?" I asked with a laugh. "You realize that the weather is only getting colder as the day goes on."

She shrugged. "When I was pregnant with Helene, all I wanted was iced coffee, but I gave it up entirely. I still can't get enough of it."

"That makes more sense." I blew on my coffee, which was still too hot to drink. "I'm so glad you messaged. I was just dealing with the worst parents. Their daughter walked out of my class, and now, they think they're going to come after *me*."

Katherine practically cackled. "Yeah, good luck with that. Don't they know who you are?"

"They're small town, small-minded, and they don't seem to care."

"Well, thank God you and I will be back in New York City in a week then." Katherine held her drink out to cheers, and I knocked mine against hers with a wince. But she was too perceptive and latched on to the twitch. "What is it? Aren't you ready to go back? Don't you miss the city streets and the crisp smell and shopping and food and excitement on every block?"

She was projecting. That was for sure. She clearly missed New York, which made sense since she'd grown up there. But I'd grown up here with wide-open spaces and cotton fields and family. It wasn't as easy to go back to that life even if it was *my* life.

"I am. I do miss the city."

"But..." Katherine offered.

I shrugged, not sure how to even begin to explain.

"Let me guess...a boy?"

"Am I that transparent?" I asked with a laugh.

Katherine grinned wickedly. "I can read people." She leaned forward. "Now, tell me about this boy."

"Isaac. You met him at the charity event a couple weeks ago."

"Oh, right," Katherine said, tapping her lip. "He was good-looking, quiet type, body of secrets."

I shook my head in disbelief. "Well, yes. You *can* read people, can't you?"

"That's my superpower."

"We dated for three years in high school and broke up

when I left for New York. Now, I'm back and he has a daughter and we…kind of hooked up last night."

Katherine arched an eyebrow. "That is a lot. But… what do you think is going to happen in a week? He has a daughter? That's serious, Peyton."

"I know," I whispered.

"We're going back in a week."

"I know."

"So…it's just a fling?"

My wince must have told her otherwise.

Katherine reached out and touched my hand. "Your life is in New York. You're at the top of your game. You're a principal dancer." Her voice held more awe than I'd heard from her before. "Are you really considering giving all that up for some high school ex?"

I didn't know. Was I? Was I even considering that? I'd had to make the choice once before. I didn't want to have to make it again. But I knew the day was coming up quickly, where I would have to choose…and I had no idea what I would do.

*M*y mom kissed me on the cheek when I came home late and only managed to cock an eyebrow but not ask any questions. "I'm glad you had a good night."

"Thanks, Mom."

She grinned at me again and then hopped in her car.

"Aly Cat, are you ready to go to school?"

"I don't want to go, Daddy," she said, coming out of her bedroom with her arms crossed. She was dressed in jeans and a sweater with no shoes or jacket or gloves or anything.

I sighed. "I know you don't want to go, but it's only a half-day. And when I pick you up, I'll have a surprise waiting."

Her eyes lit up. "What is it?"

"If I told you, it wouldn't be a surprise."

"But, Daddy, how will I know what to wait for?"

I laughed. "You're too smart. How about this? If we get

your shoes on and finish getting you ready to get to school, then I will tell you."

"Okay!" she said and ran back to her room in a hurry.

I followed her, helping her pull on her tennis shoes and then a hat and gloves. We found her jacket in the hall closet and put that on next. Then, we grabbed her backpack and the lunch that my mom had made for her the night before. Thank God for that.

"I'm ready! Tell me now!"

"Once we're in the car."

She huffed exaggeratedly and flopped down on the ground. Aly was a wonderful kid, but she was still a kid. And she threw a tantrum like a pro. Tears sprang to her eyes, and she started sobbing in the middle of the floor. I checked my watch. We were going to be late if we didn't get moving.

"One," I said quietly but firmly.

"Daddy, no!" she cried.

"Two."

"Don't do it," she said, coming up to her feet. She wiped her tears and glared at me. "Don't say it."

I waited, wondering if I'd have to get to three. Waiting out her tantrums was such a nightmare. I'd never been prepared for the worst parts of parenting, but it wasn't parenting if you didn't get the good along with the bad. I should just be thankful that, more often than not, Aly was a dream kid.

"Are you better now?" I asked her.

She crossed her arms. "You'll tell me in the car?"

I forced down the smile threatening to take over. "Once you're in your seat."

She grumbled and then followed me outside.

I buckled her into her car seat in the back, and then once I was in the front—thankfully with a few minutes to spare—I told her, "Peyton is going to come over to help us bake cookies later."

Aly's eyes widened to saucers. "Miss Peyton is coming here? The Sugar Plum Fairy can bake?"

I laughed as I drove us to her school, only a few blocks away. "Yes. Would you like that?"

"I'd *love* that. I love Miss Peyton. She's who I want to be when I grow up."

A lump formed in my throat, and I didn't know what else to say. I let Aly ramble the remaining few blocks. Then, I parked out front of the school and unbuckled Aly. She gave me a big hug and kiss, her tantrum forgotten, before darting toward the entrance.

"Love you, Daddy!" she cried over her shoulder.

"Love you, Aly Cat," I yelled back, knowing, one day, she'd find that embarrassing so I'd hold on to it as long as I could.

I breathed a sigh of relief as I pulled away from the school. She'd had bigger meltdowns. In the early days, I'd had no idea how to even deal with them, but giving in usually only made it worse. Putting my foot down was much more difficult though. We'd both learned and grown through it.

The Wright Construction parking lot was empty on Friday morning, save for Morgan's black Mercedes—she never took time off—and Jordan's sleek silver Tesla Model S. He'd let me drive it once, and it was the most beautiful, unnerving ride I'd ever taken. It sat low to the ground, made practically no sound, , and jolted forward like a bucking bronco when I barely touched the accelerator. I'd known then and there that it wasn't for me, but it was still gorgeous.

I headed inside and took the elevator up to my office. It was a large corner space on one of the top floors. I dropped my keys, wallet, and cell phone onto the desk and then powered on the computer. With the added soccer complex project on my desk, I'd never felt more behind. It would have been great to take this day off with the rest of the staff, but if Aly had a half-day, then I needed to use it to play catch-up.

I'd completely lost track of time when I heard a knock on my open office door.

"Hey, man. Didn't anyone tell you that you had today off?" Jordan asked with a grin as he lounged against the doorframe.

"Someone might have mentioned it."

"Are you as much of a workaholic as I am?"

I laughed. "No. I don't think anyone is more of a workaholic than you. I just had to finish up all this paperwork for the soccer complex that I'd neglected to focus on. I didn't want it looming over my head all Christmas break."

Jordan nodded. "Seems reasonable." He looked down at the Rolex on his wrist. "It's almost noon. Do you want to grab some lunch before diving back into this?"

"Shit, is it really noon?" I checked the clock on my computer and cursed again. "Where did the day go?"

"Time flies when you're having fun," Jordan said in his characteristic sarcastic tone.

"I'd be into lunch, but I have to pick up Aly soon. She only has a half-day for her last day of school," I told him as I set my office back to rights.

I'd have to try to stay late sometime next week to finish all of this. My mom was going to love that.

"Rain check then," he said. "I'll see if I can drag Morgan away."

I glanced up at him with an incredulous expression. "Good luck with that."

He smirked and then stepped into the office, dropping into the seat in front of my desk. "Yeah, you're probably right. Seems unlikely. I don't know how Patrick deals with it."

"I think he likes it."

Jordan shrugged. "To each their own." His phone beeped, and he checked the message, jotting out a response before stuffing it back in his suit coat. "Went on one date with this girl, and now, she texts me five hundred times a day."

"Oh, how hard it is to be you," I said with a laugh.

"True story. Speaking of relationships," he said, leaning forward with his elbows on his knees, "how are things with the girl you brought to the party last night? You two seemed really into each other." Heat crept up my neck, and I tried to hold back my smile, but I must not have succeeded because Jordan laughed and said, "That good, huh? Where did you two meet?"

"Well, we dated in high school."

Jordan raised his eyebrows. "And you're back together? Damn."

"Peyton is different. She's a professional ballerina in New York. She left right before our senior year."

"Huh. And so she...lives in New York?"

"Yeah. She's here for *The Nutcracker* for the Lubbock Ballet Company."

"And...she's going back to New York?"

I sighed. "She is. After Christmas, she has to be back in the city. But we're just trying to make the most of it while she's here. She's actually coming over to hang out with me and Aly this afternoon."

This time, Jordan looked actually alarmed. "You're letting her meet your daughter?"

"They've already met," I said, hating the defensive tone in my voice. "Aly is in *The Nutcracker*, too."

"Right, but...okay, when I was young, my parents split up for two years. We lived with my mom and saw my dad on the weekends. He started dating a few other women, and he introduced us to them all right away. Then my parents got back together." Jordan looked away as if the story still brought painful memories. "I mean, I was glad that they worked it out, but he never seemed to care how his dating life affected us."

My mind whirred to life...and fear replaced what I'd thought was going to be a fun and light afternoon. "That must have been hard."

"Yeah. I remember it more than Julian, but it sounds like this thing with Peyton is serious. And I like you, man. You and your little girl. I'd think about how she would take this if you started introducing a new woman into her life."

"Right," I said, speechless.

Jordan groaned and got to his feet. "Hey, I didn't mean to drop all that on you. You know what's best for your daughter and your relationship."

"No, I'm glad that you told me. I want things to be serious with Peyton but not at Aly's expense."

"Maybe it'll all work out," Jordan said. "What do I know? I'm terrible at relationships." He held his phone up as proof.

I laughed with him, and then we exited the building together. He clapped me on the back before heading for his Tesla, and I wandered to my truck. Jordan might have been nonchalant about it afterward, but...his words stuck with me.

Would bringing Peyton around Aly hurt her? Was I going to damage my child by introducing her to someone I was dating when she might just leave in a week?

Aly was the most important person in my life. I would never jeopardize her. She'd already lost her mother. I didn't want her to suffer more because of my choices.

19

PEYTON

After coffee with Katherine, I went back to the studio and spent the rest of the morning digging through all of Kathy's paperwork. It felt like an endless job. I wasn't used to doing paperwork. My feet and body itched to get into the studio and dance the rest of this away. But I had the show tonight, and I was supposed to meet Isaac and Aly to make cookies.

Of course, I wasn't entirely sure it was a good idea anymore. I couldn't get Katherine's words out of my head. I was returning to New York in a week. My life was there. I was at the top of my game. Could I give that up? Would Isaac even want me to?

I shook my head to clear my mind, but it did nothing. All my thoughts just swirled and swirled and swirled. There was only confusion and hopes and wants and then reality. A constant push and pull. One I was very familiar with from a decade ago. I checked the time. Thirty minutes before I needed to leave, and I made a snap decision. I didn't want to sit and obsess for another thirty minutes.

So, I left the rest of the paperwork and grabbed pointe shoes and a pair of shorts out of my bag. Once I changed, I stepped into the dimly lit studio. No one else was even here right now. I had it all to myself.

I knew my body well enough to start with a quick warm-up to get my muscles moving. A series of *pliés*, *tendus,* and *relevés* before stepping away from the barre and into the middle of the floor. With no music, I just let myself glide across the floor. Until I realized I was in the middle of a seventeen-minute solo that I'd performed two years ago before a packed audience at Lincoln Center. Aside from *Swan Lake*, it was the hardest performance of my life. The sheer energy and technicality had pushed me to my limits.

Truthfully, I hadn't even been sure that I'd be able to get it right by the time we were performing. Seventeen minutes was an unbelievably long time to be alone onstage without a break. I had to be engaging. I had to be breathtaking. And I had to be perfect. Story of my life.

At the end of the final turn sequence, I landed in a soft fourth position, my chest heaving. I was definitely out of shape for that number, but I'd finished it.

And then I heard soft applause from the studio entrance.

I jumped, whirling around to find Bebe standing in the doorway. "Bebe, you scared me."

Her smile was electric as she held her brown toe shoes. "Sorry. I had a half-day, and I wanted to work on that turn section." She took a step forward, wringing her shoes. "How did you *do* that?"

"How long were you standing there?"

"Long enough," she said with awe in her voice. "That was the most beautiful thing I've ever seen in my life."

I laughed softly and wiped sweat from my brow. "Believe me, I've performed it much better. I'm afraid I'm a bit out of shape for it."

"No, you looked so...happy. As if you'd found your place in the universe."

That was exactly how I always felt while dancing. "That's what you look like, too, you know?"

Bebe flushed and looked away. "I don't know. I'm never going to be as good as you."

"Not with that attitude. The differences between the best dancer in the world and you are two things: experience and confidence. Experience, you're going to have to earn just like anyone else. Confidence...that's all you, Bebe."

She stood a little straighter. Her head tilted upward. "Thank you, Peyton. I'm glad that you're here in the studio. I've never seen anyone stand up to Katelyn the way you did."

I sighed. Ah, the crux of the problem. I headed over to where she stood and put my hand on her shoulder. "Katelyn only has as much control over you as you let her."

"She thinks I can't handle this just because I'm new."

"Do *you* think that?" I asked.

"Sometimes," she whispered. "But I won't give up."

"Good. Never give up, or she wins."

Bebe nodded. "Thanks, Peyton. I guess I'll get to work on that turn sequence."

"That's a good idea. And then maybe, next week, we can talk about summer intensives." I arched an eyebrow.

"Oh," she whispered. "You think so?"

"You're good enough. You just have to believe it."

She nodded. "All right. I trust you."

I swallowed back the lump in my throat as I left her to practice for our final weekend. I changed back into my jeans and headed out to my borrowed car. The wind had really picked up. It was beginning to look dangerous out here. I wondered if we were going to have to cancel the show tonight if it snowed.

I plopped down into the car and slammed the door shut against the whistling wind. I put the heat on full blast and checked my phone to make sure Isaac was home.

Peyton, change of plans. I don't think it's a good idea to bake cookies. We'll see you at the show tonight.

My mouth fell open. What the hell? What had changed?

Of course I was nervous about getting too involved with him when I was leaving so soon. But that made me want to spend every minute alone with him. Not...this.

Is everything okay?

My stomach twisted, even as I sent the text message. Because clearly...everything was not okay.

Everything is fine. I don't think we'll have enough time, and Aly has been throwing tantrums all day. Trying not to reward her bad behavior.

Okay, that sounded reasonable. If that was all this was. But something told me that this wasn't all that it was. I couldn't shake it.

See you tonight.

I was frustrated, but it wasn't like I could argue with him. He was a dad first and foremost. We'd been living in some kind of alternate reality, where his mom and sister were taking care of his kid so that we could have time together. But it wasn't always going to be like that. And I was leaving in a week. Did I even have a right to be upset?

With a sigh, I drove away from the studio. Piper and Blaire were at work, and I didn't feel like being alone right now. So, I went to the one place that I knew someone would be home—*Abuelita* Nina's.

The wind buffeted against me as I rushed for the door. I glanced grimly up at the darkening sky as I knocked. I didn't wait for her to answer before stepping inside.

"*Abuelita*?" I called.

"Peyton?" she asked, stepping out of the kitchen, holding a bowl in her hand.

"*Hola, Abuelita*. What are you making?"

"It's *Las Posadas, mija.*"

A sigh escaped my lips, more like a groan than anything. I'd forgotten. I didn't celebrate back in New York. Even though I knew a few Mexican Americans who hosted traditional Las Posadas parties in the city, it just wasn't the same. Not compared to being with my *abuelita*.

For the nine days before Christmas, we celebrated the journey Mary and Joseph had taken to get to the inn with food and a party and a traditional piñata. As a child, I had looked forward to it every year. My mom and *abuelita* would be in the kitchen all week, making tamales and atole. Then, us kids would get to knock down the star piñata—a symbol of the star that guided the Three Wise Men—filled with candy and treats. Then, we'd end with a Mexican hot chocolate and *buñuelos*.

Abuelita must have recognized the pain and confusion written on my face. "Come. I just made a fresh pot of hot chocolate."

"Chili powder?" I asked hopefully.

"I know which child you are," she said with a laugh.

I followed her into the kitchen and slumped into a seat at the breakfast nook. She put a mug in my hands, and the hot chocolate, sweet and spicy, tasted better than any I could get in the city.

My *abuelita* returned to her kneading, and we sat in silence for a few minutes.

"*Buñuelos*?" I asked hopefully.

They were a traditional Christmas sweet treat— round, fried discs sprinkled with sugar. When they were still warm, I could eat them by the plate full.

"I was making the dough ahead of time, but I can fry up a few for you."

"*Gracias.*"

"Now, tell *Abuelita* what is wrong."

"I'm leaving in a week."

"That is a problem. You should stay."

I chuckled. Of course that would be her solution. "I can't stay. My entire life is in New York."

"No, your entire life is here," she said, adding a disc to the frying pan. "Dance is there for you."

I frowned down into my hot chocolate. I hadn't ever considered it like that, but she was right. My family was here. Isaac was here. My childhood was here. New York held a lot, but mostly, it had dance.

"I don't want to give up dancing," I told her. "But...I think something is growing between me and Isaac again. I don't know what to do."

"If you're leaving in a week, then you break it off. He's been through too much, *mija*." She waved a spatula at me. "But if you find a compromise, then you make it work. If it's real, it will work."

"It feels real," I whispered.

"I left your *abuelo* in Mexico to start a new life here. I was all alone. I only knew *mi amiga*, Ana María, who helped me cross over to Texas. I just knew that there was more here than I could give *mi familia* back in Mexico. Eventually, he came up here, too, but I hadn't known if he would. I hadn't known if he thought it would be worth it to come to America for new opportunities. He'd had to decide if it was real, if he could compromise."

I heard what she was saying, what she was telling me.

That this was my choice. I could choose to go back to New York, to never compromise my love of dance for anyone else, as I had done at seventeen. Or I could find a way to make it work.

"Now, no more worrying." She plopped a plate of freshly fried *buñuelos* in front of me. "Eat. This will make everything better."

20

PEYTON

*C*omfort food always made me feel better.

And hanging out with *Abuelita* knocked the jitters out of me. We laughed through the rest of the afternoon as I helped her prepare her famous rice pudding. Then, I got ready for the performance in front of the vanity where I'd learned to do makeup, and I headed back to the performing arts center.

I hadn't heard from Isaac again. Though I knew he'd be dropping off Aly. Despite the hours I spent with *Abuelita*, I still wasn't sure what to do. If I could compromise. I just needed to talk to Isaac. It was the elephant in the room. We'd ignored it as long as we could, but we couldn't ignore it any longer.

As soon as I stepped into the mayhem that was the studio before a performance, I locked eyes with Katelyn. She looked smug and haughty, as if she had won something. But I didn't have time to deal with her. She was a product of her parents and nothing else.

"Peyton, there you are!" Nick, the executive director, said. "Can I speak to you for a moment in private?"

"Of course," I said.

I glanced back at Katelyn once more, and she was grinning like a cat watching a mouse walk into her trap. Well, this should be fun.

We stepped in my office, and Nick shut the door. "Sorry about all this."

"No problem. What's going on?"

"Kathy called me this morning after the Lawsons confronted you. I just wanted to let you know that you have the full support of the LBC and the board. I spoke with them this afternoon. Apparently, the Lawsons had already spoken with a few of them, but I consulted with some of the students about what happened in that class. They all had the same story—your story—and the board agreed to back you."

"Well, that's a relief since I did nothing wrong."

"Agreed. Unfortunately, the Lawsons are powerful lawyers and a powerful family in Lubbock," he said and stuffed his hands into his pockets. "Too long, they've had influence over our institution. It's honestly satisfying to tell them to shove it."

I laughed and touched his shoulder. "Thanks for having my back."

"Anytime. Now, go do your thing. I love watching you perform every night. Such a vision."

"Thank you," I said with a flush. "Hearing that never gets old."

Nick winked at me and then hustled back out into the lobby. I stepped out with a satisfied smile.

"Looks like someone was finally put in their place," Katelyn singsonged from the end of the hall.

Bebe rolled her eyes. "Whatever, Katelyn."

She snatched the Clara dress from out of Bebe's hands. "I don't think you'll need *this* anymore."

The sheer audacity of this girl.

I took a step forward, all my rage at this entitled brat coming to the surface. But before I could even reach her, Bebe snapped the dress back out of her hand.

"You have to earn this, Katelyn." Bebe moved into Katelyn's personal space and raised her chin. "And we all know you haven't earned it."

Katelyn opened her mouth, likely to say something nasty, but Bebe turned on her heel and strode away, unconcerned by Katelyn's behavior.

I didn't move a step closer. I just watched it all go down in awe. Bebe. *Bebe* had done that. She'd found her own confidence and turned on Katelyn. I couldn't even believe it. Had *I* helped her find the person inside herself to do it? Either way, it was amazing.

"All right, everyone," I said to the crowd of kids. "Let's get into places. Finish warming up. The show starts in fifteen minutes."

Katelyn looked like she was going to say something to me. I waited with a raised eyebrow, and then she darted away, defeated. Good. She could be an incredible dancer one day, if she learned that life wouldn't give her everything she wanted. Like Bebe had said, you had to work for it.

My eyes skimmed the rows of excited children. This was our last official weekend for *The Nutcracker*. Three shows this weekend and then Lubbock Ballet Company's Christmas Eve Spectacular show, which was a special matinee event for underprivileged children in Lubbock. All tickets were donated by parents and sponsors, and our charity director worked with the city and local elementary schools to promote the arts. It was everyone's favorite show. It had been mine when I was here as a kid.

But I couldn't deny that as I was looking over the kids, I was waiting to see a shock of red hair and to hear Aly's excited voice. Isaac wasn't usually this late. Aly should have been here already.

I checked my phone one last time, but I didn't have any missed calls or texts.

"Peyton, let's get you into costume," one of the backstage managers said.

"Of course." I followed after her. "Have you seen Aly?"

"I haven't. Let me send someone to look for her." The manager stopped a runner dressed in all black and asked her to find Aly. "Now, costume."

By the time I was once again in a tutu, the runner had located Aly, and all was well. Except that Isaac had never texted me, which was strange. The night before, we'd stayed up all night in his hotel room, and now, he was ghosting me?

That didn't feel like Isaac. My stomach churned over the possibilities, but I kept coming back to this being impossible.

In the wings, I swallowed hard as I moved up and down on pointe to work my ankles. I couldn't accept that. He hadn't been acting like a guy on the prowl. Isaac was kind and thoughtful. He loved his job and his family. He was a terrible liar. Always had been. There had to be an explanation.

"Peyton, everyone is set," Cassidy said, nodding at me.

I took a deep breath and nodded. "Showtime."

Dance swept me away.

I'd seen *The Nutcracker* a thousand times, and the magic of it all still transformed me. The Sugar Plum Fairy role was challenging, and yet muscle memory took over when I was out there. I never faltered. I never wavered. It was just me and the music and this perfect role filled with joy.

My heart beat in my chest as I took my final bow to a roaring audience—something I never tired of—and then ran gracefully into the wings.

Just as the curtain fell for the last time and I hit my wing, my foot collided with something backstage. I gasped as I stumbled forward, and before I could catch myself, I landed hard...on my knee.

"Fuck," I spat, crushing the tutu as I lay on my back and tried to remember my breathing exercises. It was the only way I'd gotten through the worst of the pain the first time.

"Peyton!" Cassidy gasped. She fell to the ground next to me. "Are you hurt? What can I do?" She looked up at my partner, Reginald, and yelled, "Go get some ice!"

"I'm fine," I got out through gritted teeth. "I'm fine."

"You're not fine. You're crying."

Was I?

I wiped tears out of my eyes and came into a sitting position. "It's okay. Just shock," I told her. "What did I trip over?"

Cassidy left me for a moment and came back with a pointe shoe. "Who the hell would have left this here?"

I held my hand out for it. The shoe wasn't the traditional satin pink. It had been dyed a deep brown, and the initials *BB* had been inked into the shank.

"Bebe would never be so careless," Cassidy said.

"No," I agreed, "she wouldn't."

Reginald rushed back over with ice then. I waved him off and let him help me to my feet. My knee throbbed, but I wasn't reinjured. It wasn't any worse than my normal pain after a performance. Or maybe...just a little worse. But I certainly wasn't going to show that to anyone backstage.

"We have someone we need to speak with," I told Cassidy.

"You think someone did this on purpose?"

I gritted my teeth. "Unfortunately."

"Do you need help to walk, Peyton?" Reginald asked.

"No, I'm fine, Reggie," I lied. "Thanks."

"Should I get Nick?" Cassidy asked in a hushed whisper.

I nodded. "That would be best."

I headed into the backstage area and waited. My knee was killing me, but not a single person would know it was the case. The younger kids filed out first and then the professional company members, who hugged me as they left. Which just left the high schoolers, who always dawdled longer than the rest.

My feet were planted, and the shoe was in my hand when the group of them came out of the dressing room. Bebe among them this time.

I held my hand up. "Bebe, I believe this belongs to you."

Bebe gasped. "You found my shoe! Where was it?"

"It was in my wing," I told her, handing it back.

"What?" she asked in utter confusion. "Why would it be in your wing?"

"That's an excellent question," I said firmly, eyeing the rest of the company. "Does anyone else know why Bebe's shoe would have been in my closing wing?"

Half of the girls looked at each other or down. The other half looked confused. Katelyn held my gaze. Not saying a word.

"Do you know anything about Bebe's shoe, Katelyn?"

She shrugged. "If she can't keep up with her things, that's not my fault."

"Katelyn, did you put Bebe's shoe in Peyton's final wing?" Cassidy asked in horror.

"No!" she gasped. "How dare you accuse me!"

A few of the other girls bit their lips.

"She could have been seriously injured," Cassidy said in her motherly, disappointed tone.

"We know you did it," I said.

"You have no proof," Katelyn spat at me.

I smiled. Gotcha. "But I don't need proof, Katelyn. We're not in a court of law. And judging by your friends' discomfort, they knew full well what you were doing with Bebe's shoe. You're out."

"Excuse me?" she gasped.

"You're out of the company."

"You can't do that!"

"Actually, she can," Nick said. "The consequence for harming a fellow company member, let alone one that we have on loan from the New York City Ballet, is expulsion. If the artistic director says you're gone for your behavior, then I agree with her."

Katelyn's mouth dropped open.

But I stepped forward. "Unless...you want to apologize to me and Bebe for what you did."

Katelyn snapped her mouth shut, and then said, "I didn't do anything."

"If you apologize, then we could put you on probation. You would still dance the last three shows of *The Nutcracker*. You'd still perform in the spring." I leaned in. "No one would have to notify Joffrey that their summer intensive student tried to harm a principal dancer."

Her jaw was set. For a moment, I really thought she was going to tell us all to fuck off and storm out. Such was her picture-perfect life that she never, ever thought there would be consequences for her actions. That she could get away with everything because her parents were high-powered attorneys and life had always gone her way.

Then, she burst into tears, shocking all of us.

"I'm sorry, okay? I'm sorry. I shouldn't have taken Bebe's shoe, and I didn't want to hurt you, Peyton. I just...I just...I'm sorry. I felt it all slipping away, and I lashed out." She swiped at the big tears running down her cheeks. And Lord help us all, she was even pretty when she cried. "I won't do it again. I swear. Please don't kick me out. Please don't tell Joffrey. Ballet is all I have." She looked so young and vulnerable. Like a kid and not the entitled brat she'd been acting like since I got here. "Ballet is all I have," she repeated.

I nodded. "I accept your apology. So long as your actions prove it, going forward." I looked to Bebe. "Do you accept?"

Bebe nodded. "Yeah. Ballet is all I have, too."

Katelyn looked up at the girl she'd been harassing all season. "I really am sorry."

Bebe shrugged and put an arm around Katelyn. "Maybe we could try to be friends from now on?"

"Yeah," Katelyn said, wiping at her eyes. "I think that'd be good."

I let them all pass and then slumped back against the wall.

"You did excellent, Peyton," Cassidy said warmly.

"Truly," Nick agreed. "You handled that like a professional."

"Thank you. I'm just...glad she apologized. For a second, I thought she'd dig her feet in."

Cassidy nodded. "Me too."

"Hopefully, that's the last we hear from the Lawsons," Nick said, patting me on the back.

"Are you sure you're okay?" Cassidy asked.

"Fine," I said quickly. "I'm just going to change. I'll be out later."

They nodded, melting back into the roles for the company while I hobbled into the now-empty backstage and collapsed onto a chaise, letting the tears finally roll free down my cheeks.

21

ISAAC

I paced back and forth outside of the studio exit. Peyton hadn't left yet. I checked my watch again. It was nearly an hour after the show had ended. All the kids had left a half hour ago. I'd even seen a few of the runners leave ten minutes ago.

When Cassidy finally came out, I stopped her with a smile.

"Hey, have you seen Peyton?"

"I thought she'd already left! She might still be backstage. We had a little...drama tonight with the high school girls," she said conspiratorially. "You're free to go back there if you want to see her."

"Thanks, Cassidy," I said, entering the backstage area.

I'd been back here dozens of times while we were building the facility, but once it had come to life, it was strange to see it so...dead. Even the janitorial staff had finished cleaning up the stage. I could only hear them moving around out in the auditorium, looking for any trash.

I searched everywhere, except the women's dressing room before realizing I was going to have to go in there. Where else would she be? She hadn't snuck out in front of me. I'd been waiting for her.

With a sigh, I rapped on the door. "Peyton?"

"Isaac?" her voice called out in confusion.

"Is there anyone else in there with you?"

"No."

"Can I come in?"

She paused. "Yes."

I pressed open the dressing room door and found Peyton still in costume, lying on a chaise. Her eyes were red and puffy, as if she'd been crying.

"What are you doing here?" she asked.

"I was waiting for you."

"Where's Aly?"

"She left with my mom at intermission. I wouldn't have even let her dance if it hadn't been a responsibility. She'd been a nightmare all day."

"I'm sorry."

"Not your fault. She had been bad in the morning, and then she got in trouble at school. So, I told her we had to cancel baking cookies with you. Then, she turned into a nightmare and had to go into time-out. It was a whole thing." I stepped forward. "Why aren't you out of costume?"

She blew out a heavy breath and looked at the ceiling. "We had...an incident with Katelyn."

"Cassidy said there was high school girl drama."

"Yes. She planted one of Bebe's shoes in my exit wing. I tripped over it." She sighed. "And landed on my knee."

My eyes darted to her knee. Now that I knew, I could tell that it was swollen. "Your...hurt knee?"

"Yes."

"Shit, Peyton. Are you okay?"

"Honestly? I don't know. It hurt when it happened, but I ignored it to confront the girls, and now, I'm not sure I should move."

I dropped down before her and took a look at her knee. "Did you tear it again?"

She shook her head. "No. It's not that bad. I'll probably be fine if I ice it and take some medicine and rest. It only hurts worse than normal. I just don't know how I'm going to drive home."

My eyes flicked up to hers. "Worse than *normal*?"

She bit her lip and looked like she wanted to kick herself. "Um..."

"Your knee still hurts? I thought you'd recovered?"

"I did. I mean, I mostly did." She winced. "I'm, like, ninety percent better. I did PT and I work out and the pain is almost always gone."

"When does it hurt again?" I asked in horror.

She gulped. "I don't know. When I dance..."

"Peyton...all you do is dance."

"I know," she whispered, closing her eyes and letting tears fall down her cheeks. "I can't quit. I can't give it up, Isaac. I just love it too much."

"Okay. Well, let's not talk about quitting. Let's get you home and see how bad it actually is. Maybe it's just inflamed because you danced on it for a half hour."

She nodded. "All right."

I helped her sit up, and together, we stripped her out

of her costume. As much as I wanted to admire her body, I kept myself clinical. She needed help, and I was here for her. No matter how beautiful she looked right now.

She tugged a shirt on over her head as I went to carefully lower her tights. She hissed slightly as I pulled them over her knee. It was definitely swollen. But not as bad as it had looked when obscured by the pink material. I stripped her shoes off along with the tights, helped her into a pair of sweats, and then her winter coat.

"Where's your bag?"

Peyton pointed it out, and I grabbed it, slinging it over my shoulder. Then, I leaned down and slipped my hands under her body.

"What are you doing?" she asked, her eyes wide.

I hauled her into the air. She gasped, and I saw pain cross her face.

"Is this okay?"

She nodded. "Yeah. Thank you."

I carried her back out through the empty backstage, across the lobby, and to my truck, gently placing her on a foot at the passenger side.

"Sorry you had to carry me," she said.

"It's fine, Pey. You don't weigh anything," I said with a chuckle. "Plus, I couldn't just leave you there." I wiped a tear off of her cheek. "I'm going to get you home safe."

"What about my car?"

"We'll leave it. It'll be fine. We can pick it up tomorrow if we have to."

She nodded, grabbing my jacket and pulling me into her. I wrapped my arms around her shoulders and held her tight to me.

"I thought you were ghosting me."

I kissed her forehead. "That was my fault. I'm sorry."

"I kept telling myself you weren't that kind of guy, but then..."

"Then, I acted like a jerk," I told her. She blinked up at me. "I just...freaked myself out. Why don't I get you home, and we can talk then?"

She nodded. "I'd like that."

Peyton hobbled into the passenger seat, and as we pulled away from the performing arts center, snow started falling. She laughed with all the enthusiasm of a child and watched the snow with wide eyes.

"I never get tired of that first snowfall. It's all sludge in New York afterward, but the first snow...it's magic," she whispered.

I reached across the console and took her hand, lacing our fingers together. She didn't pull away. Instead, she leaned over and rested her head on my shoulder. We drove the rest of the way back in comfortable silence.

Once we were back at Piper's, I helped Peyton into the living room and headed to the fridge for ice.

"There's a note here from Piper," I told her. "*Staying at Bradley's tonight.*"

Peyton rolled her eyes. "So much for *we're just friends.*"

I laughed. "Sounds right. Where's Blaire?"

"She went to Ruidoso with her family for the weekend. They have a cabin in the mountains."

"Going to be a good weekend to be there. Perfect snowboarding weather," I told her as I came back over with an ice pack.

Without a word, I wrapped it around her knee and

then went in search of medicine. She washed down some ibuprofen with water and finally rested back on the couch with a sigh.

"Looks pretty bad out there," I said, peering through the windows at the snow.

"Do you need to get back to Aly?"

I rolled my eyes. "You know my mom's fear of driving in snow. She told me not to move from where I'm at until it all clears."

"But...you could probably make it before anything happens, and you're in a truck. You know people drive in snow all over the US?"

"I know that. Tell that to my mom."

Peyton laughed. "I sometimes forget your mom's irrational fears."

"She's great, but...well, you know."

"I do. Remember that time that we were supposed to go skiing in Santa Fe, but your mom was too worried it was going to snow?" She giggled again. "At the ski resort."

I took a seat across from her with a grin. "I do remember that. God, that was so long ago."

"It was," she whispered.

So many memories between me and this beautiful woman. A lifetime of memories in those three years.

Today, I'd let myself get all caught up in the what-ifs that I hadn't even talked to her. It had been a mistake. I wanted another lifetime of memories with her. Because when we were together, it was the only time that felt completely right in my life. I loved Aly with all my heart, but she was my kid, not my partner. And I hadn't even realized how much I'd missed having one until Peyton stumbled back into my life.

"About today…"

She held up her hand and looked down at the ice pack on her knee. "It's fine, Isaac. If you were with Aly and she needed you, then I get it."

"It's more than that. Aly was a struggle today, but…I'm falling for you all over again."

Her head popped up in surprise. "Isaac…"

"I know that it's only been a few weeks, and I know that you have to go back to New York. I know all of these things. And when we're apart, I stress about them and worry that I'm making the wrong choice. But when we're together, Peyton"—I moved to sit next to her, taking her hand—"the world is right."

She swallowed. "I feel the same way."

"I don't know what we're going to do. You're leaving for New York in a week. Your job is there. Your life is there. I couldn't ever ask you to give that up. I couldn't do it when I had you when we were kids, and I'd never think to ask now." I kissed her hand. "But I don't want to walk away from this either."

"Me neither," she whispered. "But how…how is it even going to work?"

"We'll figure it out," I told her honestly. "If we want it to work, we'll figure it out."

"Okay," she agreed hesitantly.

"I know it's not going to be easy, but this…*you* are what I want, Peyton Medina."

"Yes," she said as I brought my lips to hers. "You're what I want, too."

"We have one more week. Let's just take it one day at a time. After Christmas, we can figure out how to make this work."

She nodded and brought her hand back up to my jaw, pulling me in for another kiss. "In the meantime," she whispered against my lips, "we have the house to ourselves."

"Your knee…"

She laughed. "Maybe I can try to be sexy after I finish icing."

I drew her lips against mine one more time. "You're always sexy. And I'm here to take care of you…anything else is just a bonus."

"I'd like to take you up on that bonus."

Fuck, I wasn't just falling for this woman. I was in love with her. Unequivocally.

And I let the rest of my fears and consequences dissipate as she tossed the ice aside and drew me toward her. Who was I to deny her anything?

22

PEYTON

*T*he snow fell thick and heavy all night and through most of the day Saturday. And while this much snow wouldn't have been a big deal in New York, Texas wasn't equipped for it. To my dismay, we had to cancel the show Saturday night.

It ended up being a blessing in disguise since I needed the extra day of rest. Especially considering my... extracurricular activities with Isaac.

Luckily, by the time the Sunday matinee show rolled around, the roads were clear, and my knee was back to normal. Which wasn't a hundred percent, but the swelling had all gone down, and I could walk again without pain. I was sure dancing was going to make it worse, but there were only two more shows in Lubbock, and I wasn't ready to hand it over to the understudy.

Isaac had gone home Sunday morning when the roads were clear, promising to see me at the soccer game that night. Since I had no car, Piper agreed to drive me to the studio.

"Remind me again why you don't have a car," Piper asked as we headed that direction.

"Remind me again why you were snowed in with Bradley."

She huffed, "I wasn't *with* Bradley. I was just at his place."

"Uh-huh," I said disbelievingly. "Is it because Blaire was gone, so she couldn't talk you out of it?"

"No!"

I laughed at my sister. "I love you."

"I love you, too," she grumbled.

She dropped me off at the front entrance, and I felt the normal swell of excitement right before I went onstage. That dissipated as soon as I saw who was waiting for me—Angelica and Bart Lawson.

I should have anticipated it. Of course I couldn't hope that Katelyn would actually be a bigger person and let it all go. That she'd realize the consequences of her actions. Instead, she'd brought in the big guns. Great.

Katelyn stood just behind them with wide eyes. It wasn't the vindictive, smug look I was used to from her. I met her gaze for the briefest moment, wondering what she was thinking, before turning to her parents.

"Hello, Mr. and Mrs. Lawson," I said with the biggest smile I could muster, ignoring the stares from the rest of the performers who had already arrived for the show. "Thank you for dropping Katelyn off for the show this afternoon. Are you going to stay to watch? She's a lovely flower."

"You know why we're here," Bart growled.

"You tried to kick our daughter out of the show!" Angelica snapped.

They had an audience now. I had confronted Katelyn in front of her peers but not the entire show. This was humiliating.

"Why don't we go inside my office to discuss this?" I said graciously.

"We're not going anywhere with you. I'll have you know that we plan to sue you and this company for what you've done to our daughter," Angelica said, arching an eyebrow.

"Really?" I said without inflection. "Well then, I believe there's nothing more that I can say, and I'm going to have to ask that you vacate the premises."

"You can't kick us out," Bart snapped. "We have a right to air our grievances."

"I'm sure that you do. However, threatening legal action will only get you dismissed from the building." I gestured to the door. "Have a nice day."

"You—" Angelica said, taking a step forward.

"Stop!" Katelyn yelled. She silenced everyone, but her gaze was on me. "Everyone, just stop. This has gotten *completely* out of hand."

"Katelyn..." her father said gently.

"No, Daddy. You two need to stop. I want to stay in the company. I want to go to Joffrey this summer."

"We know, baby. We're making sure that happens," her mother said.

"No, you're making it worse," she ground out. "You don't have to sue everyone who disagrees with you. Just... go watch the show."

"But you deserve better than this treatment," her father said.

Katelyn met my gaze and nodded. "Then, I'll earn it. Maybe next year, I'll be Clara."

Her parents looked flabbergasted by her outburst, but Katelyn just masterfully shuffled them toward the door and shut it behind them. Her shoulders heaved, and everyone was still watching.

"All right, show's over," I said, clapping my hands. "Let's get back to work."

Everyone breathed a sigh of relief and went back to what they had been doing. I walked over to Katelyn and put a hand on her shoulder.

"You too," I said gently.

She looked up at me, and something like understanding passed between us. Katelyn wasn't going to completely change anytime soon. I could see that in her stubborn expression and the way she couldn't quite say anything about what had happened. But as she headed back to the dressing room, I had hope that she'd get there.

Even though we still had one more show on Christmas Eve, everyone was celebrating the end of the official run. Kathy had even shown up with her teeny-tiny baby for the performance.

She pulled me into a huge hug. "Thank you *so* much for taking over. I've heard having you here for a month has been transformative. You make a spectacular artistic director, just like I knew you would."

"Thank you, Kathy. I just worked with what you had already established."

"I heard about what had happened with Katelyn, too." Kathy winced. "Sorry about leaving you with that land mine."

I laughed. "It's fine. We worked it out. Or at least, I think so."

"Well, good. I should have known they'd take advantage of a transitional period. It's like they were trying to destabilize a government." Kathy dramatically rolled her eyes. "Anyway, here. Hold Lily."

I took the little dumpling in my arms and cooed over her as Kathy went to have five whole minutes alone.

"You're holding a baby," Isaac said, appearing before me.

"Oh my God, you scared me." I rocked the baby, hoping to slow my racing heart.

"Sorry about that." He put his finger out, and Lily wrapped her little hand around him like a vise grip. "She's so cute and squishy. God, I forgot how little they are."

"Do you want to hold her?"

He nodded, and I passed Lily off to him. He held her like she was the most precious thing in the universe. And he was much better at it than me. It was clear that he'd held a baby many a times before. My heart melted all over as I imagined him with Aly like this.

"You're a natural," I said, running my finger over the baby's chubby cheek.

"Lots and lots of practice," he said with a laugh. "Are you still planning to meet me at the game tonight?"

"Yep. I'll be there."

"Aly is coming."

"Oh, really? I thought you normally had someone watch her."

"Normally...I do. But Sutton and Jennifer said they could manage. So, I thought you could all hang out."

"I'd like that," I admitted.

I wanted to be more involved with his life. Figure out where this was going. If it was possible for this to even work.

Kathy appeared back again. "Oh, look at you!" she gasped when she saw Isaac. "God, I am such mush when I see a man holding a baby."

Isaac chuckled and offered Lily back to her mom. "She's cute."

"I sure think so," Kathy said. "Are you two going to the after-party tonight? Nick is hosting it at his mansion at, like, eight o'clock."

"I'll be there after Isaac's soccer game," I told Kathy.

"Aw, it's just like high school," Kathy said with a wink. "Isaac, you are more than welcome to join her."

"I'm not sure if I'll be able to make it since that's Aly's bedtime, but I'll see if I can."

"Good seeing you two." She hugged me one more time, pinched Isaac's cheek, and then headed back out.

He laughed and shook his head. "I'm going to grab Aly. I'll see you at the game."

"Sounds good," I said as he drew me into a hug.

His lips found mine, and I debated on dragging him

into an empty dressing room. But of course, we couldn't act like high schoolers even if he made me feel young and carefree.

"I'll see you later." He kissed me one more time and then disappeared to locate his daughter.

I headed back to the dressing room and changed out of my tutu. Luckily, my knee had held up through the show. In fact, the day of rest seemed to have helped it more than I'd thought it would. It hadn't been too bad during the show and I could walk just fine now.

I shouldered my dance bag and went to check my messages as I headed out of the studio. I froze on the threshold when I saw that I had five missed calls from Annabelle, the assistant to the production director for NYC Ballet as well as a few from the production director and artistic director.

My heart thudded in my chest. What the hell had happened?

I clicked the first voicemail.

"Peyton, hey, it's Annabelle. We're in a tight spot. Can you call me back as soon as you get this? ASAP!"

Well, shit.

I needed to call her right away and find out what had happened. This couldn't be good. I hadn't really heard from anyone in the month since I'd been gone—besides regular check-in stuff because we were all friends. Nothing like this kind of bombardment.

With a sigh, I hustled into my car to get out of the cold and dialed Annabelle's number.

"Hey, this is Annabelle."

"Annabelle, it's Peyton. What's going on?"

"Oh my God, Peyton, I'm so glad that you called. Disaster struck. Lauren just had an emergency appendectomy!"

"What?" I gasped. "Is she okay?"

"Yes, she's fine. She's going to be fine. The doctor said that they got to everything in time. She'll make a full recovery, but she can't be on her feet for two to four weeks."

My eyes bugged. "That's awful. I'm glad she's okay, but oh my God."

"I know. We all had a meltdown. It happened right after the show today."

"Wow."

"And she was supposed to dance the Sugar Plum Fairy for the rest of the week. I've reached out to everyone we have who's rehearsed the role, and literally, no one is free. Could you by any chance hop on a plane and be back in New York for tomorrow's performance?"

My mouth went dry. *Tonight.* They wanted me to fly out tonight? But what about Isaac's game and the after-party and the Christmas Eve performance? Crap, what was I going to do?

The ballet was my job. It was my dream job at that. It was all I had ever wanted growing up. And now, I had it, and I'd thought that I'd be able to have everything else I'd ever wanted, too. A life. A family. But...that just wasn't possible.

My career and life were back in New York. They weren't here in Lubbock. This was who I had been, and it had been nice for a few weeks to think that everything could work out...go back to how they had been. But I'd just been deluding myself. There was no way this could all work out.

I wasn't even going to get to have Christmas here with my family. That was how it was...how it would always be.

As much as I wanted it to work with Isaac, neither of us knew how it would happen. We'd been avoiding it more than we'd really discussed it. We'd "figure it out." But what was there to figure out?

I was going back to New York. He was staying here with Aly. That was the truth. The unavoidable truth.

"Sure," I finally said. "Yes, I can be there. I have to move some things around, but I can make it."

"Thank God! You're a lifesaver. I don't know what we'd do without you," Annabelle gushed. "Okay, I'm going to buy your ticket right this second. First class from Lubbock to New York City with a layover in Dallas. It looks like the latest flight is nine fifteen tonight. Think you can make that if you hurry?"

"Yeah. Lubbock is small. I only have to be there forty-five minutes early."

"Ah, the joys of small towns," Annabelle said. "I already have your frequent flyer number. This should be in your inbox in a few minutes. Thanks so much for this, Peyton."

"Of course. It's my job."

"There's a ten o'clock rehearsal to make sure that we have you all set to perform. Is there anything else you need from me?"

"No. That's all, Annabelle. Thanks."

"You're the best, Peyton. See you tomorrow."

I hung up and then rested my head on the steering

wheel. I was leaving. I was flying back to New York tonight, a full five days early. No Christmas with my family. No Christmas with Isaac and Aly.

I wanted to cry, but somehow, I couldn't even manage that. A part of me had known this was coming all along. Now, I just had to find a way to tell Isaac.

"*A*ly, please don't make me say it one more time. If you want to go to Daddy's soccer game, you have to put your shoes on."

"Fine," she groaned and stomped back to her room.

My mom stood by with an amused look on her face. "You hated shoes, too."

"I'm sure this is cosmic torture for how I was as a kid."

She laughed and patted my cheek. "You're doing just fine."

"Thanks," I said with a sigh. "You sure you still want to go to the game? Sutton and Jennifer said they'd watch her. Plus, Peyton will be there."

"Bah," she said, waving me off. "I'll be there for you. As if I ever get tired of watching you do what you love."

"Thanks, Mom," I said, kissing her cheek.

The doorbell rang in that moment, and I raised my eyebrows.

"Wonder who that is."

"I'll go check on Aly and her shoes," my mom said,

walking toward Aly's room as I headed for the door.

I pulled it open and was surprised to find Peyton standing in the doorway. A smile split my face, and I wrapped my arms around her. "This is a pleasant surprise. I thought we were meeting at the soccer complex."

She frowned, backed out of the embrace, and looked down at her feet. "Isaac..."

She was in fitted black leggings, a tank top, and a cardigan. Her heavy peacoat thrown over top. Her hair was still in her tight ballet bun. She usually let it down right when she got home. But then I looked past her and saw...Piper's blue Jeep. With Piper idling in the driver's seat.

"What's going on?"

"Isaac, I...I don't think this is going to work."

My fingers clenched the door. "What do you mean? What isn't going to work?"

She gestured between us, swallowing hard as she met my eyes. There was torment in her irises. She didn't want this.

"Why?" I gasped out. "Why are you saying this?"

"I got a call from New York. They need me to come home tonight. Their Sugar Plum Fairy had emergency appendix surgery, and no one else can come in to perform."

"So...you're going to go back to New York? There's literally no one else?"

"No one with enough experience. Not for what the tickets cost," she said softly.

"But you don't want this. You don't want to go back to

New York already. We were supposed to have Christmas together. We were supposed to—"

"I know," she forced out. "I know what we were supposed to have, Isaac. I know."

"Then why?"

"This is my job," she said softly, gently. "I don't want to hurt you, and I know we said we were going to find a way...but what way is there? How could this work?"

"I don't know," I said, straightening. "I thought we were going to figure that out together."

"We were. But the more I think about it, the more impossible it feels. I'm in the studio eight-plus hours a day. I have shows constantly. I'm teaching and training and performing. Not to mention, volunteer work and banquets." Helplessly, she held her hands out before her. "My life is in New York. It's not here."

"I'm not going to stand here and tell you not to follow your dream or to give up your career for me," I said carefully. "I didn't do that when we were seventeen, and I'm not going to do it now. But I want you to think about this before running off and abandoning what we have." I reached out and took her hands. "I love you, Peyton."

Tears came to her eyes, and she drew in a ragged breath. "Isaac..."

"I love you. I've always loved you. I will always love you. Here. In New York. Wherever. You are the person that I want. If you don't feel the same, then fine. Go back to New York and walk away from this." I drew her in closer, swiping a tear from her cheek. "But if you do feel the same way, Peyton, please just give me a chance."

She closed her eyes and let the tears fall freely. "I'm

sorry, Isaac. I'm sorry."

"Don't be sorry. Be mine. Be here with me. Be there with me. Just be mine." I pressed a kiss to her mouth. "I know that you love me."

"Please don't make this harder than it has to be."

"I can't make it easier on you. I don't want you to go. I can't imagine you walking out of my life again."

"I know," she whispered. She opened her big brown eyes, and I saw the resignation in them. "I don't want to leave. I don't want to end this. But ballet is my one true love. It's the only thing that has always been there for me. And it's calling me back home. So, I'm going back to New York…and I don't think we can do this long distance. You have a daughter to think of."

"I do. I love Aly. I want what's best for her. And what's best for her is me falling madly in love with you."

"How would it even work?" she asked, swiping at her face. "You come up on weekends with your daughter? I almost never have time off. A few days here, a few days there. That's not a life. That's not fair to you or Aly."

"So, it's better to walk away from love?"

"No," she gasped. "It's better to face reality. The last month has been a dream, Isaac. One I never wanted to wake up from. But we're not kids anymore, and we have to face the fact that we can't be together when we're two thousand miles apart!"

I stood stock-still as her words hit me. She was telling the truth. She really believed this. I'd known that she was going to go back to New York, but I'd thought she cared enough to want to at least try.

"You're really going," I muttered.

She nodded her head. "I am. I'm sorry."

"And we're just over? You can walk away this easily?"

"It's not easy," she whispered. "I don't want to do this."

"Then don't."

"But it's real life, Isaac. In the fairy tale, I give up my big, fancy job, and I move back to my small town and marry my high school sweetheart. In real life, I go home. And we both learn to live with the heartbreak."

Everything went cold. Inside and out. Her words felt like she'd stabbed me in the heart.

She stepped forward, pressing one more forlorn kiss to my lips. "I do love you, Isaac. And I'm sorry that I came back...that I'm hurting you all over again."

Then before I could reach for her and beg her to stay, she darted back down the front walk and hopped into Piper's Jeep. They pulled away while I stood there at the front door, staring at them in shock.

It wasn't until Aly charged back down the hallway and wrapped herself around me that I broke away. I picked her up and held her as tightly to me as I could.

"Daddy, I can't...breathe," she said while laughing.

"Everything all right?" my mom asked with worry creasing her forehead.

I carried Aly into the living room. "Peyton left."

"Oh dear...back to New York?"

"Yes."

"And you two?"

"Over."

"Isaac...I'm sorry."

Everyone was sorry. So sorry. But that didn't make her any less gone.

24

PEYTON

"D o you want to talk about it?" Piper asked as she drove me to the airport.

"Not really," I whispered.

I stared out the window, brushing the tears off of my cheeks and watching the bare cotton fields pass by.

"I wish that you were staying."

I sucked in a deep breath. My lungs hurt. My body felt brittle. What was I even supposed to say to that after what I'd done?

"Me too," I managed to force out.

But I didn't want to give up ballet. I couldn't. It was ingrained in me. And I didn't see another option.

Piper sighed and merged onto the highway. "I'm sorry about Isaac."

"Yeah."

"Peyton—"

"Just...don't, Pipes, please," I muttered, diving into my own sorrow. "It was hard enough the first time."

Piper nodded, reaching out and taking my hand.

"Everyone else understands, you know? We'll be sad not to have you here for Christmas, but we get it."

"Thanks."

"I didn't really expect you to stay anyway."

I swallowed and choked back another sob. No one had expected me to stay. Only Isaac had hoped for it. Only I'd let him think it was possible. Even though it was never possible. Now...we were over, and I was walking away from Lubbock with another broken heart.

Piper drove her Jeep up to Departures and hopped out to pull my suitcase out of the trunk. I hoisted my dance bag over my shoulder. It hurt, knowing that I wouldn't get to perform for the last show in Lubbock. Kathy had been completely understanding. They had an understudy in place, who was anxious to play the role. But I'd *wanted* to perform that final show.

"Don't be a stranger," Piper said, yanking me into a hug.

"Of course not. I'll text you when I land."

"Good. Maybe I can come up this spring when you're in between shows. We can eat those amazing dumplings at that place we went to in Chinatown. And oh! Cuban from that place near Times Square. Also, what about that Ethiopian place?"

I held up a hand, managing a small smile. "I get it. You're coming to see me so that you can eat."

"What else is there to do?"

I snorted. "I'll miss you."

"Me too. You're always welcome back. I have a spare room for a reason. It's yours if you want it."

"Thanks, Pipes," I said, hugging her one more time

before taking the suitcase out of her hand and heading into the small Lubbock airport.

I reluctantly handed the bag over and then breezed through security. My plane was already boarding. I put in earbuds to block out the world and let a T-Swift breakup song wash over me.

What was I going to do? This...this wasn't supposed to happen. I wasn't supposed to have fallen in love again. Not with Isaac, who was wonderful and had an amazing kid and...it just couldn't work out. Now, my heart felt like it had been put through a shredder. And I had to go home and dance and act and pretend like everything was fine. When it wasn't fine.

But I knew it would hurt us even more if we ripped the Band-Aid off slowly. If we tried long distance, it would never work. The flights between New York and Lubbock were outrageously expensive. Plus, there were no direct flights. It wasn't fair to make either of us live our lives in the air. To live our lives separate but desperate to be together. We'd break down just from the impossibility of it. I'd rather leave us on a moment of pure happiness than risk destroying something across two thousand miles.

True to Annabelle's word, I had a first-class seat that I could sleep in and took advantage of that the best that I could.

When I finally landed back at JFK, it was a freezing nineteen degrees, and I was ill-prepared for the sharp drop in temperature. Lubbock was cold but not biting.

I wrapped my peacoat tight around myself, glad that my luggage was the first out, and then hailed a cab to the city. Thankfully, at three forty-five in the morning, there was miraculously little traffic, and we made it back to my apartment in record time. I paid the driver and stepped out onto the sidewalk. My gaze lingered over the dirty street and flickering lamppost and the barred gate that led up to the apartments overhead.

This was home. And it had never felt less like it.

I let myself inside and checked my mail, which still had a bunch of junk in it despite diverting it for the month to Piper's place. Then I lugged my suitcase up the six flights of stairs since no one had bothered to install an elevator.

My apartment was thankfully untouched. The building was completely safe, but there was always that fear in the pit of my stomach that it would be ransacked when I left. It had happened to a friend or two too many when I first moved here, and I'd never been able to shake the feeling.

I closed and locked the door behind me, leaving my suitcase to deal with tomorrow. I only had about five hours before I needed to be in the studio again. Something that I normally looked forward to, but now, I just couldn't fathom it.

Without preamble, I plopped down into my bed and stared out the one window, which looked out over a fire escape on another building. I should have fallen right asleep. My eyes were heavy with exhaustion. My body felt as if it had been run over. Except my brain wouldn't stop. And I needed it to just stop.

"Oh God," I gasped.

Suddenly, it felt as if I had been cracked down the

middle. Split open like an autopsy that popped my ribs open to reveal all the gooey organs within.

And then I was crying. Big, racking sobs that I couldn't hope to contain. Just pain upon pain upon pain. I lay there, completely subsumed by my own grief.

I'd thought it was hard to leave Isaac the first time.

I had been wrong.

This was much worse.

I must have fallen asleep at some point because I woke up to the sound of my alarm blaring from my phone. I startled out of bed and moved in a daze to get ready for rehearsal. There was no food in the house, but I couldn't imagine stomaching it either.

So, I just pulled my hair up into a shoddy bun, flyaways haloing my head, and flagged down a cab to take me to Lincoln Center. Normally, I wouldn't waste the expense, and I'd just take the subway, but I was too numb for that today.

It wasn't until I was inside, lacing up my pointe shoes that I thought to ask who I would be performing the *pas de deux* with this week. I knew next week would be with André. We'd planned it so that we were together for the last week. He was my favorite partner.

But as soon as I heard the booming voice, I knew that I wasn't just unlucky; I was doomed.

"Peyton, you're home early," my ex, Serge, cried, bending down to kiss me on both cheeks.

I scrambled to my feet, flustered. This was...not good.

"Serge, I didn't realize you were dancing as Cavalier this week."

"Of course. I was there when Lauren had her..." He vaguely gestured to his stomach, as if unaware where the appendix was located. "I helped her into the ambulance."

"That must have been traumatizing."

"No," he said with a dimpled smile. He was a head taller than me with thick, curly black hair and the musculature that showed the extra effort he put into the gym. I wished he'd put that extra effort into our relationship, but what did I know? "I'm great under pressure."

"And modest," I joked flatly.

He chuckled. "You were always so funny, Peyton. I missed you while you were away."

Had he? Seemed doubtful.

"I don't need to be in the studio long," I told him. "I could do this role in my sleep. Let's just make sure that we're in sync, and then we'll go from there."

He looked at me in surprise. "You want to just do a few run-throughs and leave?"

"Yeah?" I asked, uncomfortable by his shock.

"Texas must have changed you, butterfly," he said, brushing his hand across my skirt.

I stepped back at the familiarity. I didn't like this.

"Normally, you would run this number all day until you were blue in the face."

I shrugged. "I took a red-eye. I'm tired."

"Ah," he said, unconvinced. His eyes took a measure of me that I didn't appreciate. "Then let's begin."

The artistic director came through in the middle of our rehearsal and applauded our efforts. "Lovely, Peyton.

I can tell the time away has been rejuvenating. You're simply effervescent. I cannot wait to see you onstage." His eyes turned to Serge. "Keep working on the lift sequence. Use your *plié*."

Then, he was gone.

I was breathing out heavily. Had Lubbock rejuvenated me? I didn't feel like I was dancing any differently.

"Typical," Serge muttered.

"What?"

"Use your *plié*," he grumbled. "As if I haven't heard it a million times."

I knew better than to give him a critique. He never took criticism well—in ballet or outside. So, I just let it hang between us.

"Do you want to go one more time?" I asked.

He shook his head. "No. Let's run it before we go on."

"All right." I tugged off my shoes and walked to my discarded bag. I guzzled down the bottle of water. My stomach grumbled noisily, reminding me that I hadn't eaten that day.

Serge leaned against the wall next to me. "Do you want to go get lunch?"

"Thanks, but I think I'm going to grab something on the way home and see if I can get a few more hours of sleep before tonight."

He reached out and grasped my hand before I could flee the studio. "Hey, it's really good seeing you." His thumb trailed along my palm, and I pulled it back.

"Sure. See you tonight."

"Since we're both here," he interrupted, "you know... for Christmas, maybe we could do something together?"

His eyes were wide and endearing. God, how had I ever fallen for him? I knew what he wanted. He wanted me to be a pushover and let him back into my life. He wanted to have a Christmas lay and go back to being indifferent to everything. I was only interesting right now because I'd been gone. And likely...because my mind and heart were set elsewhere. Now, I was a challenge.

"No, thanks. I'm going to get sushi and veg out. Thanks for the offer though," I said with a polite smile and then left him gawking at my refusal.

God, I missed Isaac.

I looked down at my phone as I left Lincoln Center behind. No messages. Of course, I couldn't expect him to text me after what I'd done. I clutched it tight to my chest to keep myself from making that first move.

It was easier this way...better. Even if everything felt like it was crumbling down around me. A destruction of my own making.

25

ISAAC

"**G**randma! Look what Santa brought me!" Aly cried as soon as my parents entered the house.

"Wow, Aly Cat," my mom said. "Is that Elsa and Anna?"

"Yes!" Aly said triumphantly. "It's what I wanted."

"That's so lucky."

My dad patted me on the shoulder as he came inside and then took a seat on the couch to survey the disaster that was my home post-Christmas presents. My mom busied herself with Aly as she explained every single toy she'd received.

Annie filed in last. "Hey, big bro. How are you doing?"

I shrugged and shut the door. Peyton had been gone for five days. I hadn't heard a peep from her. Of course, I didn't expect to. She had made herself clear. We were over, and whatever we'd had was just a fantasy. Not real life.

"We brought over the rest of the presents," my mom said.

Aly clapped. "More presents! Yay!"

"At least she's having a good day," Annie said thoughtfully.

"Had to make it special for her. She deserves it," I told her.

If nothing else, life with Aly was exactly the same. That was the thing about being a parent. It was a twenty-four/seven kind of job that never ceased or changed, no matter what happened in your life.

No matter if I was a fucking mess and just wanted to drink whiskey and fall into oblivion.

"Come into the kitchen with me," Annie said.

She guided my shoulder that direction, and I followed her easily.

"What's up?" I asked, pouring myself another large cup of coffee.

"I found something while I was at Mom and Dad's this morning."

"Oh yeah?" But when I turned back around to look at her, I frowned at what was in her hand. "Why do you have that?"

"Well, I was going through our old stuff. Do you know how much junk you still have at their place? You should really go through it."

"Get to the point, Annie," I muttered.

She laughed and then bit her lip. "Anyway, I found a bunch of your stuff from high school, and there was this picture."

I knew which one it was before she even passed it to me.

Peyton and I were sixteen. I'd just gotten my first car, which was a hulking beast of a truck that only worked half the time. We drove it down to the lake at Ransom Canyon to visit friends. Someone—I couldn't even remember who—took a picture of us standing in front of the truck with the lake and the canyon in the background. We weren't looking at the camera, but at each other. I had my arm around her shoulders. She was laughing at something I'd said, and I...I looked at her like she was sunlight after a dark winter. She had been my very existence.

I set the picture facedown on the counter. "You probably shouldn't go through my things."

"Isaac, come on," Annie muttered. "You didn't even read the back."

"I don't need to," I said.

I ignored my coffee and went to the cabinet where I held the whiskey instead. I poured myself a shot and then downed it without looking back.

Of course I knew what the back said. Peyton had printed the picture and given it to me to keep in my locker when we went back to school for junior year. I'd looked at it every day for a full year.

I love you. I'll always love you. Nothing can come between us.

—Pey

The message felt futile now. It had seemed true when she gave it to me as a kid, but now...it was obvious that things had come between us. Were still coming between us. And it was pointless.

"It's over, Annie. I don't need reminders about it right now," I muttered.

"You know, I liked it better at the soccer game on Sunday when you were pissed off."

"Why is that?" I poured another shot.

Annie yanked it out of my grasp and tossed it into the sink. "Because at least then, you *felt* something. You were mad. You ran around the field like you were on fire. You demolished our opponent. I've never seen anything like it."

"Great. I'm still a good soccer player, even when I'm fucked up."

"Stop it," she snapped, and I met her hardened green gaze. "I get being upset. I get wanting to mope around about this, but the person who wrote this?" She grabbed the picture and waved it in my face. "She's still out there, and she still loves you."

I snatched the picture out of her hand. "The person who wrote this left me sixteen years ago." I dropped the picture into the trash. "She's gone, Annie. She's gone."

Then, I brushed past her and back out into the living room to watch my daughter open a few more presents that she didn't need.

▲

Christmas wasn't a good day.

Of course, it was just like any other Christmas. And I was glad to have it with my daughter and my family. We opened presents and cooked dinner and celebrated the holiday. But...I was in a dark place.

My mom seemed so worried about me that she even offered to take Aly for the night. But if I didn't have Aly, then what would I do with myself?

I knew that I sounded depressed about what had happened with Peyton. And I was. I didn't know how to stop it. I didn't know how to make it better without her. I'd just started thinking that there was something else in this life other than my daughter's existence.

Now, I was back at square one.

I kissed my parents good night and ignored the concerned looks from Annie.

"Night, Grandma!" Aly said, hugging my mom. "Night, Grandpa and Aunt Annie."

Aly gave everyone sloppy kisses, and we waved from the front door as they drove away.

"Daddy," Aly said as I closed the door.

"Yes, sweetheart?"

"Can I stay up with you tonight?"

"No, honey, you have to go to bed."

"But I want to stay up with you. I promise to be a good girl." She reached up and took my hand in hers and smiled brightly. "You look sad, Daddy. I can cheer you up."

I swallowed back the lump in my throat and then nodded. I hoisted Aly up into my arms. "All right, you win. Just tonight, because it's Christmas, you can stay up with me. Why don't we turn on a movie?"

"*Frozen!*" she gasped.

"What?" I said in mock shock. "Do you like *Frozen*?"

"Daddy, don't be silly," she said with a giggle.

I carried her back into the living room and set her down while I turned on *Frozen*. For a solid hour, I just sat with my daughter as we watched the movie for what had to be the thousandth time this year. But I didn't even care. It was just nice to have her snuggled up against me.

Aly yawned as big as I'd ever seen her, and I could feel her weight start to slacken as she leaned into me. I had a feeling she'd fall asleep on me out here. She'd probably still be up at the crack of dawn tomorrow.

"Daddy," she whispered through another yawn.

"Yeah, honey?"

"Is Miss Peyton still going to come over to make Christmas cookies?"

My heart constricted. We'd had to cancel cookies when Aly had her nightmare day last week. But...she still thought it was going to happen. How did I begin to tell her that Peyton was gone?

"I don't...I don't think so, honey," I told her gently.

"Are you sure?" Her big brown eyes looked up at me.

"Yeah, I'm sure."

"Why not?"

"Peyton went home."

"We could go to her house," Aly suggested as if it were that easy.

"I think that's a great idea, Aly Cat, but Peyton doesn't live here. She lives in New York City. She's really far away, and it's not easy for her to come and make cookies with you."

Aly stuck out her bottom lip. "Well, tell her to come back."

"I can't," I whispered.

"Then...can we go to New York City, Daddy?" Aly asked through another yawn.

"I don't think so."

"Well, I'd like to go see her." Her eyes fluttered closed. "She's really nice and she dances and we should make cookies. I want to be just like Miss Peyton when I grow up."

I clenched my jaw and tried not to let the wave of pain blast through me. Aly meant nothing by it. Not like my parents or Annie. She wasn't trying to sway me or make me do something stupid and impossible.

Aly just...loved completely. And in this short time, she had fallen in love with Peyton as only a child could. She didn't know her as the woman who had stolen her dad's heart. She had no clue that I was madly in love with Peyton. Just that she didn't want her to be gone. She didn't think it was possible for someone to just disappear on her.

Even though Aly had lost her mother, it had happened when she was a newborn. In some way, she never really knew the loss of Abby. She'd never really known loss at all. And in her stubborn five-year-old mind, she just didn't want Peyton to go.

And neither did I.

But how in the hell could I fix this—for me and for Aly?

"Great show tonight, Peyton," my dance partner, André, told me as we came offstage from the final bow.

"Thanks! You too."

My knee twinged slightly, but I couldn't deny the incredible feeling of being back in Lincoln Center performing on stage at the Koch Theater before an enormous, enthusiastic, full audience. And dancing with André was way better than the last few performances with Serge. He really couldn't take a hint.

"I think some of us are going to get drinks out if you want to come with," he offered.

"Sure. I'm down," I told him with a smile.

Anything to get me out of my apartment. All I'd done in the eight days since being back was dance and obsess over leaving Lubbock. Going out with my friends would hopefully help me to stop thinking so damn much.

I popped a few ibuprofens before changing into jeans

and a sweater to combat the cold. New York was in one of those fluke freezing temperatures. It was all supposed to clear up for New Year's and be something like seventy-five degrees when the ball dropped. So confusing.

But right now, it was chilly.

André waited near the back entrance with his boyfriend, a group of flowers, and a few snow soloists, who all gushed over my performance. André slung an arm around his boyfriend's shoulders and winked at me as we departed as a group. I get lost in the cluster of people as they all discussed the show as only ballerinas could.

A handful of people hung out at the exit, mingling with other dancers and waiting for significant others. André invited a few more of the performers out with us, and we lingered in a gaggle as they decided who was going.

I rubbed my hands together and blew into them to try to keep them warm. Hanging around outside was a bad idea for my knee. As soon as it got cold, I knew it would get stiff, and I'd pay for it tomorrow. I should probably go home and ice it. But the thought of being alone in my apartment was just not appealing.

"Come on. We need to get moving," I told André.

He waved at me and continued his conversation with one of the other dancers. I rolled my eyes and pranced up and down on the balls of my feet to keep the warmth in.

Just then, I felt a tug on my peacoat. I turned around in confusion.

"Miss Peyton! Miss Peyton! You did beautiful!"

I gaped at Aly Donoghue standing before me, holding an enormous bouquet of roses.

"Aly?" I gasped. "What are you doing here?" My gaze shifted over the crowd. "Where is your dad?"

"We wanted to surprise you!" she said, stuffing the flowers in my arms. "Did it work?"

I pulled her tight against me. "Yes! It absolutely worked. I cannot believe that you're here."

"But you're glad, right? Daddy said that you might not be happy to see him."

"What? Of course I am. And I'm so glad to see you, too," I told her truthfully.

"Aww, Peyton, who is your admirer?" a flower asked. "She's adorable."

"This is Aly," I told her with a smile. "Could you tell André that I had to bail?"

"Sure thing. No problem." The flower fluttered her fingers at Aly. "Have a good night, cutie!"

"Night!" Aly said. She took my hand in hers and then tugged me away from my group of friends. "Come on. This way. Dad was right over here."

"He let you wander off alone?" I asked in disbelief.

"No, he could see me the whole time. He's not far. Remember, it was a surprise!"

And I was surprised. Oh my God, what was even happening? Aly could not be here right now. Isaac most certainly couldn't be here right now either. Not after how I'd left and what I'd said.

Then, I saw him. I stopped in my tracks. Isaac was here. He was standing right before me with Aly still trying to yank my arm out of the socket to move us closer.

"It's okay, kiddo," Isaac said, ruffling her hair. "You did a good job."

Aly dropped my arm. "I did it just like you'd said, Daddy! I surprised her!"

"Good girl." He kissed the top of her head, but then his eyes moved back up to mine. "Hi, Peyton."

"Isaac, I can't believe you're here."

God, I couldn't stop staring at him. How was he here? How was this happening?

"It was a little last minute," he conceded.

"But...what are you doing here?"

He grinned sheepishly, but then his confidence returned, and he stepped closer to me. "Aly wanted to bake cookies."

Of all the excuses he could give, that wasn't the one I'd been anticipating.

And I couldn't help it. I laughed. "Cookies?"

"Yes, Miss Peyton!" Aly cheered. "We were supposed to make cookies. And then Daddy said that you came here instead. But I still wanted to make cookies."

I looked between them in awe. Of course they hadn't come here just to make cookies. No matter how excited Aly seemed by the prospect. I could tell what they'd really come for, just from the look in Isaac's eyes. They'd come for me.

Wasn't that what I'd been moping around about for the last week anyway? I'd wanted to see them. I definitely hadn't wanted to leave them. I just didn't know what Isaac thought was going to happen by showing up.

"Well then, we'll have to make cookies, won't we?" I said to Aly.

She beamed. "Yes!"

"How long are you staying?"

"A little up in the air," he admitted. "I wanted to talk to you first. I couldn't just let you walk away without fighting for you, Peyton."

A chill ran up my back at the statement. I hadn't thought it was possible for this to work. And yet here he stood, proving me wrong, proving that he wasn't just going to let me go.

"You think fighting will fix this?" I asked curiously.

"That's why I'm here."

And he looked so damn confident, standing there in a suit with his black winter jacket, his hair gelled to perfection, and those green eyes reminding me of just why I'd fallen in love with him. Not to mention, the overeager five-year-old at his side, who wanted nothing more than to spend time with me.

He'd flown all the way here. I might as well give him a chance to explain.

"Okay," I huffed. "Where are you staying?"

He winced and ran his hand back through his hair. "Well, we came in last night and got a hotel for a night in the city. We left our luggage there after we checked out. Since we weren't sure if we were going to be staying, I didn't want to get another night. It's New Year's, you know?"

"So...everything is a million dollars?"

"Basically."

"Always practical," I told him with another laugh. "Come on. Y'all can stay at my place. It's not much, but it's free."

"Thank you," he said with a smile. He turned to Aly. "What do you think, Aly Cat? Should we go see Peyton's apartment?"

"Yes! And then cookies!" Aly cheered.

Her enthusiasm was contagious. I should have felt off about him coming all the way here after I'd dumped him, but all I felt was...relieved. Maybe I'd been hasty about the whole situation. I'd just reacted, knowing that two thousand miles was an impossible distance and dance took over my life. I could barely have a relationship with someone here in the city, who danced with me, who I saw all the time.

But after seeing Serge again, maybe it had been our relationship and not all relationships. He was selfish and self-centered, and everything had revolved around his wants and needs. With Isaac, things weren't like that. We were equals. Plus, he'd flown all the way out here at the last minute to prove me wrong.

It had to be worth pursuing.

⁂

Their hotel was within walking distance from Lincoln Center, and after they packed up their bags again, we checked out of the hotel and took a cab south.

My apartment wasn't too far away, but the drive felt interminably long with the impending New Year's traffic coming into the city. Aly gawked at the tall buildings and pointed out every little thing that she found interesting. It was brilliant to see it through her eyes for the first time.

Isaac insisted on paying for the cab, and then we were

all on the sidewalk, looking around at the same dirty streets and iron gate over my building that I'd glared at a week ago when I got home.

"You live here?" Aly asked in confusion.

"Yep. Up there actually," I said, pointing vaguely toward the seventh floor.

"But where's your yard?"

I chuckled and opened the gate. "I don't have a yard. Just an apartment."

"Okay, but I want a dog. Dogs need a yard."

My eyes met Isaac's, and I could see he was trying to hold back his laughter.

"You're right, Aly. Dogs do need yards, but some people have dogs here in New York, and they walk them to the park."

She nodded and said, "Ohh!" as if that made perfect sense.

We climbed the six flights of stairs up to my apartment, and I let them inside.

"I know it's not much," I began.

But Isaac just waved me off. "I like it. It suits you."

I looked around the one-bedroom from his perspective. It did suit me. Everything was soft whites and blues with elaborate throw rugs and exposed brick. I loved my tiny apartment even if it had felt less like home this time than any time before it.

"Are we doing cookies now?" Aly asked in excitement, walking around and touching everything.

"Not tonight," Isaac said. "It's your bedtime. Let's get you changed and brush your teeth. I'll read you a book, and then it's time to sleep."

Aly pouted. "I'm not ready for bed."

"If you don't get a good night's sleep, then we can't make cookies tomorrow. Peyton would be really sad about that."

I stuck out my bottom lip and nodded along.

"Fine," she grumbled.

Isaac went to get Aly ready for bed, and I made up the couch with sheets and a pillow for Aly. By the time she was passed out, I'd popped open a bottle of red wine, poured it into two glasses, and gestured for Isaac to follow me into the bedroom.

I took a seat on the windowsill, looking out at the fire escape instead of up at Isaac and whatever was about to happen. I was suddenly nervous. Having him here felt... inexplicably right.

It made no sense. Isaac wasn't New York in the slightest. He had been born and bred West Texas. He said y'all and drove a pickup truck and worked on construction sites. And somehow, even here in this space, he fit in my world.

"Thank you for letting us stay after I ambushed you," he said with a laugh.

My eyes flittered back over to him. He took a sip of the wine. He'd discarded his tie at some point, and he stood in slacks and a button-up with the sleeves rolled to his elbows. He didn't seem nervous. Rather the set of his shoulders and the tilt of his lips and the steady gaze all said that he was confident and prepared for this.

Unlike me.

"I wouldn't want you staying in a tiny hotel when you could stay in a tiny apartment for free."

"You know what I mean."

"I guess I do," I said, sipping my wine.

"We should probably talk."

"Probably." I bit my lip. "Is this where you try to convince me to come back to Lubbock?"

He cocked his head to the side in confusion. Then, he set the wine down on a dresser and came over to stand before me. He held his hand out, and I took it, letting him pull me to my feet.

"Peyton, have I ever given you the impression that you should have to give up your dreams for me?" he asked cautiously.

"No," I whispered.

"I'd never ask you to leave New York or the ballet," he confirmed. "But I didn't agree with you when you left Lubbock so abruptly. I'd been considering how we could make this work, but I didn't really put it together until you were gone."

"And what did you decide?"

"That I can't live without you."

My breath caught. "Isaac..."

"Not just that, but I don't want to. We deserve our happiness, Pey, not just our dreams." He drew me in closer until we were only inches apart. "I've figured out how it will work. I'll come up on the weekends with Aly. You can come down between performances when you have time off."

"Wait—"

"No, let me finish. And then once I can, I'll request a transfer to move up to the New York office. It's smaller, but Wright is everywhere. They'll find a place for me when they can."

My jaw dropped open. "You'd move to New York?"

"For you?" He lifted my hand and pressed his lips to my fingers. "Anything, Peyton."

27

ISAAC

*P*eyton had tears in her eyes.

God, I hoped they were happy tears.

I'd meant every word of it. After Aly had fallen asleep on me on Christmas, I'd decided that I couldn't sit by and let this happen to me. If Peyton was what I wanted, then I couldn't let her be the one to have to make the sacrifices. Happiness was a two-way street.

So, I'd booked the first flight to New York for me and Aly, held my nose as I paid the insane hotel price, and purchased tickets to Peyton's show. I had no idea how it was all going to go down. But I didn't think Peyton wanted to give our relationship up any more than I did, and if that was the case, then I had a plan to fix what we'd broken.

"We can make this work," I assured her again. "I really think that we can."

"What about Aly?" she gasped.

"It'll be harder," I admitted. "I can't lie about that. New York is so much more expensive than Lubbock, and

I wouldn't have the support I'm used to with my parents and Annie. But she's five. I think she'd adjust just fine here. She'd learn to love the city like you do. And we'll fly her back to see everyone when we can."

"Isaac...I don't know."

"Look," I said, pulling the picture Annie had given me at Christmas out of my pocket that I'd saved from the trash can.

She took it from me with trembling hands. "I remember giving this to you."

"Me too. It was after we went to Ransom Canyon. You wanted me to keep it in my locker. It was a promise."

She turned the picture over. "*Nothing can come between us,*" she whispered.

"I still believe that, Peyton. It might be difficult. It might not be what we always envisioned. But for us, for you and I to finally be together, I think it's worth it. I think it's all worth it."

She clutched the picture to her chest with her eyes closed and shook her head slightly. She was going to say no. I could see that on her. All of this was for nothing. It just couldn't end like this.

"Peyton, look at me." She shook her head again. "Come on. Look at me."

She finally opened her eyes, and they met mine with pain in her irises.

"I love you. You've always had a piece of my heart, but the last month, when I was with you, was the best of my adult life. It made me realize everything that I had been missing. And that is you. If you feel the same, then please just let us *try*. Just try with me, love."

She bit her lip and then sighed. I saw indecision war on her face. But I gave her the space to think about it. It was a lot. We'd said we'd think this through, but she must have thought it wasn't possible since she'd run.

"Okay," she finally said.

"Okay?"

"I want to try."

"You do?" I asked, slightly shocked. I'd been preparing myself so much for her to say no.

"And not just that, Isaac," she said, taking my hand. "I want to come home."

"What?" I gasped.

"I've been thinking about it nonstop since I got back here. It felt right to be back in Lubbock. I loved being back at LBC. I loved being close to my family. And I loved being with you. When I came back here, everything felt... wrong." She brushed a wisp of hair off of her forehead. "The dancing is still incredible, but I'd be lying if I said that my knee wasn't getting worse every time I danced. I don't know how much longer I have, working on it full-time, even with more PT and my trainer. I don't want to go out because of a second blown knee. I want to go out on my terms."

"That makes sense," I told her. "Your knee is definitely a factor, but, Peyton, you could still be dancing professionally for another five years. I could never ask you to give that up."

"You're not asking. I'm telling you that I think if I want to walk when I get older, I can't continue the way that I am."

"Okay. Right. Injuries are no joke."

"And a small fall after tripping shouldn't cause me two days of pain."

"Fair," I admitted.

I couldn't deny that I was worried about her knee. But I couldn't see Peyton doing anything that didn't involve dance. She was happiest when she was onstage or in the studio. She was happiest in tights and leotards with her hair in a bun. That was *who* she was.

"But what will you do if you come back?"

"I don't know really," she admitted. "But I'm sure Kathy would hire me to teach at the very least. She could probably bring me in for the professional company on a part-time basis." She shrugged with her hands up. "I really haven't gotten that far. I'd have to talk to her, but I think there are options that don't involve me destroying my knee."

"Peyton, I'm really prepared to move here if I have to."

She brought her hand to my cheek. "Just the fact that you would makes me see that this is the right decision. I want to finish out the season with New York City Ballet. I'm supposed to be in a spring production and original choreography series right before summer. So, it would be six months like this, and then...then I'd retire."

I shook my head in disbelief. Even hearing those words out of her mouth was mind-boggling.

"It wouldn't be over though," she assured me. "I'd still do choreography and workshops across the country. I'd be busy. I'd have a job. It would just be a little less performing and more instructing, I think."

"Are you sure?" I asked. "I want you in Lubbock.

There's no doubt about that. Aly and I want you in our lives. But I don't want to sway you."

"You did but in the best way," she said and then kissed me.

I drew her into my arms. She tasted like a hint of red wine, and I could just dive into a vat and get drunk off of her.

This was far from what I'd ever imagined her saying. I'd been prepared to plead my case, to show her how much I wanted us to work. But then she'd surprised me by wanting to move back. Even in my wildest dreams, I hadn't thought she would do that...or ever want that.

Her fingers moved to my shirt, and she deftly unbuttoned it, pushing it over my shoulders. I let it fall to the ground as I reached for her, running my hands under her sweater to the lithe body beneath. She was perfection incarnate...and now, she was mine. She was really mine.

"I love you," I said against her skin after tugging her sweater over her head.

"I love you, too," she gasped.

My hands moved under her tank top, cupping her breasts and causing her nipples to peak.

"Isaac," she breathed. "The...the door."

Oh, right, we'd left it open. Fuck.

I gently shut it as she shimmied out of her tank and leggings. I shucked my own pants off to the side and then followed her to the bed. She tugged the covers down, and we fell into bed, kissing, touching, feeling. It was every sense all at once. So much at once. And I couldn't get enough of her body.

The way she squirmed when I trailed her hip bone.

Or the huff of breath as I kissed her stomach. The spread of her legs as my hips settled against hers.

I slipped two fingers between her lips, slicking through her wetness before pressing deep into her. She moaned softly, a sound that went straight to my dick. It strained against the fabric of my boxers as I dipped my head to lick at her clit.

"I want you," she said, reaching for my shoulders to pull me.

She grabbed a condom out of the side table as I removed my boxers. She slid the condom on me. Our eyes met as I leaned over her, positioning myself at her opening.

"I'm glad you surprised me," she whispered. "That you're here."

"I wouldn't want to be anywhere else."

She drew my lips down to hers, and I slid forward into her. She groaned against my mouth but didn't pull us apart. Our limbs were entangled and our souls connected. There was nothing between us now. Just this moment.

I picked up a rhythm as we let the last week wash off of us. Things weren't going to be easy for the next six months. Finding our footing and learning to be together was going to be all new for both of us. But it was going to be worth it to have her back in my life. To have her home.

We came together with a passion. I had to stifle my roar of pleasure to keep from waking Aly up in the living room. But it was worth it, seeing Peyton's flushed face and her beautiful sex-drunk gaze.

We both lay panting on her bed for a few minutes

before I got up to clean up. Then I came back to the bed and pulled her into my arms. "You're perfect."

She huffed a soft laugh and threw her arm over my stomach. "How long are you staying?"

"As long as you want."

"Forever?" she joked.

I kissed the top of her hair. "I have off until the fifth, but I never take vacation. So, I could probably ask off for the rest of the week."

"I'd like that," she breathed. "What are we going to do while you're here?"

I tipped her chin up until she was looking at me and grinned licentiously. "A hell of a lot more of this."

She bit her lip and nodded. "That sounds reasonable."

"Also, probably bake cookies."

She giggled. "The damn cookies."

I brushed a lock of her hair out of her face and kissed her thoroughly. "We can do whatever you want to do. As long as I am yours and you are mine."

She nodded. "Forever and always."

28

PEYTON

$\mathcal{T}$he next morning, we baked cookies, as promised.

"I think you have a little flour on your nose," I said, bopping Aly on the nose.

She gasped. "You just put flour on my nose!"

She grabbed some flour off of the counter and flung it at me, coating my shirt.

"Oh my God!" I cried, flinging more flour in her direction.

Until there was more flour on ourselves and the counters and the floor than in the cookies.

Isaac came in, freshly showered, with wide eyes. "What is happening here?"

Aly froze with a giggle.

"Flour fight," I offered, stepping toward him.

"Don't you dare," he said, using his dad voice as he backed up.

"What do you think, Aly? Does he look too clean?"

She grinned. "Definitely."

And then we rushed him. He jumped and tried to evade us, but soon, we cornered him, and both of us dove into his arms, coating him in flour, too.

"You two are in so much trouble," he said through his laughter.

Aly just giggled, and I pressed a kiss to his lips.

"This is all part of the cookie process."

"Are there actually any cookies to eat?"

"Yes!" Aly said. "Come have one, Daddy!"

We headed back into the kitchen, which was covered in flour. I pulled out a pan of cookies and switched it out with a separate tray. Aly picked one up that was still piping hot, passing it back and forth between her hands to keep from burning herself.

"Do you want icing?" Aly asked. She grabbed a butter knife and slathered white frosting on the Christmas sugar cookie in the shape of a star. Then, she coated it in green glitter sprinkles.

"Thanks, sweetheart," he said with a laugh. He took one bite and then groaned. "Oh God, are these the ones that your mom used to make?"

I nodded. "Yep. They're my great-grandma's recipe. Still my favorite. Buttercream frosting and all."

"Amazing," he said, finishing the cookie in two more bites and reaching for a second.

I completed the rest of the batch of cookies while Aly spent time decorating them all, which mostly consisted of excess sprinkles everywhere. Isaac got down on his hands and knees and cleaned the floor and cabinets even though I'd insisted he didn't have to do it. But he'd just kissed me and gotten to work.

After another hour, the kitchen was spotless, and we'd all washed up and changed into clothes to go outside. Luckily, I didn't have rehearsal until later this afternoon, so I got to show Aly and Isaac around NYC and bring them some New York Christmas magic.

We started with a horse-drawn carriage ride around Central Park. Then, we wove through the Christmas markets to grab a bite for lunch. I insisted on taking us to Serendipity 3 for a Frrrozen Hot Chocolate for dessert. The thing was so enormous that all three of us ate it together. Aly had the same love for chocolate as her dad.

"What are we doing next?" Aly asked, holding both of our hands and skipping between us. Every so often, she'd run, and we'd lift her in the air.

Isaac arched an eyebrow. "How much time do you have left?"

"Not too much, but I have one more thing in mind. Luckily, we have the rest of the week, so I can show you more things, too."

"I want every day to be like today," Aly said with such a cute, innocent smile.

My heart panged with recognition. That this little girl was falling in love with me, too. And I wanted her to. I wanted to be a part of this family. To form this new bond.

As soon as Isaac had told me that he was going to move to New York to be with me, I'd known that this was real. That my feelings about coming back to the city were more than just melancholy about a missed opportunity. And I wanted it as much as he did. I couldn't pretend like I was happy in New York, even doing what I loved. And I knew that, long-term, I couldn't dance forever. Another year with my knee in the condition it was in...and I had no idea what might happen.

At least, now, I had a plan. And I got to have the best of both worlds.

"This way," I said, tugging them down the next block.

Aly's gasp when we reached the enormous Christmas tree at Rockefeller Plaza was worth everything.

"This is the biggest tree I've ever seen," Aly whispered, wide-eyed. Then, she whirled on Isaac. "Can I have one this big for my room next year?"

Isaac burst into laughter. "I don't think that's going to fit in your room, Aly Cat."

She sighed with a little pout. "But it's beautiful."

"It is," I agreed. "It's the biggest tree in the city."

"Let's get a picture," Isaac said, pulling out his phone.

He snapped a few of Aly alone with the tree, and then I took the phone from him to grab some of them together. Then, a woman tapped me on the shoulder.

"Would you like me to take one of your whole family together?" an older woman asked.

I blanked for just a second as I realized she thought Aly was mine. But then I decided that it didn't matter. Aly *was* mine. Or at least, she would be. That was the direction we were headed. And I adored her, just like I adored her father.

"Yes, please. That would be wonderful."

I passed the phone to the woman and then went to stand with Isaac and Aly. Isaac put his arm around me, and Aly stood between us, beaming.

"You have a beautiful family," the woman said as she passed the phone back.

I looked down at the picture. *Family*. She was right. We were beautiful. More than that, it wasn't just a dream anymore. This could be reality.

"I love it," Isaac said. "We'll have to print it out."

I nodded. "I'd like that."

He pressed a kiss to my lips just as my phone started ringing.

"You get that. I'll show Aly the ice skating rink."

"I'll meet you over there," I assured him as I dug my own phone out. He was already being dragged toward the rink by Aly when I saw that Kathy was calling. "Kathy, hi!"

"Peyton, I'm so glad you answered."

"Me too. It's so good to hear from you. How is Lily?"

"An angel who can't sleep, unfortunately. But still an angel."

I laughed. "That sounds like a headstrong daughter you'd raise."

"You have no idea." Kathy chuckled. "But not why I called. Are you free for a minute?"

"Yes. I'm just at Rockefeller with Isaac and Aly."

"Isaac and Aly?" she asked in shock. "They flew out to New York?"

"Yeah, and surprised me."

"That boy. Ever the romantic."

A secret smile crossed my face. He was, wasn't he?

"Well, good. Maybe him being there will help with what I'm about to ask."

"What's this about, Kathy?"

"I'm going to officially retire from the Lubbock Ballet Company," Kathy said.

I staggered backward in shock. "Kathy!"

"I know. I didn't plan on it, but this baby is taking it all out of me. And having a little one again...it just makes me realize that I'd rather be home with her than working myself to the bone. I love the company and always will, but I think it's time for someone else to take the reins."

"I'm shocked, Kathy. I don't even know what to say."

"Say you'll come back as the artistic director."

My jaw dropped. "What?"

"I want you. Well, not just me. Everyone wants you. Everyone has been singing your praises for the month you worked as the interim here. You handled yourself with poise and confidence. You pushed the students to be better. You dealt with crises, even when it wasn't your job. And you're a damn good dancer."

"Thank you, Kathy, but...wow, artistic director."

"I know it's not right for me to ask. You have years left at New York City Ballet. You are a principal there. I don't know what kind of salary we could match, but cost of living is a big thing. There's a lot to consider, but I thought I'd shoot for the moon before landing in the stars. You know—"

But I cut her off before I could think better of it, "I'll do it."

It was Kathy's turn to be speechless.

"Kathy?"

"You will?"

"Yes. When would I start? I'm in New York through May. Would that be a problem?"

"No," Kathy said at once. "We have an interim for the

first six weeks, and then I plan to come back. We could still do that until you're back in Lubbock."

"Then, I accept."

"Are you sure? I didn't think...it'd be this easy."

"Are you trying to talk me out of it?" I asked with a laugh.

"No!" Kathy said at once. "I want you back. I'm just surprised. Does that boy have something to do with it?"

I glanced over to where Isaac stood against the railing, pointing down at the ice skaters, his daughter at his side. "Yeah, I think he does."

"Well, tell Isaac thank you from me. We're pretty lucky."

"I will. Thank you for thinking of me, Kathy."

"I'll email you with all the specifics. I can't wait to have you back in Lubbock."

"Me either," I answered honestly. Something I never thought that I'd feel.

I hung up and slid the phone back in the pocket of my jeans. Then, I headed over to where Isaac was standing with Aly.

"Everything all right?" Isaac asked.

"Kathy just offered me the artistic director spot for the Lubbock Ballet Company."

Isaac's eyes bulged. "That's incredible, Peyton. What did you say?"

"I said yes!" I gushed.

"Yes!" He picked me up and swung me around in a circle.

"Me next! Me next!" Aly cried.

Isaac laughed, setting me down to pick up his daughter and twirl her around.

"When do you start? How is this going to work?" He settled Aly against his hip and smiled wide.

"I start in May after I complete my tenure here. So, I'll move back, and I'll have a job."

"That's perfect."

"Group hug!" Aly said, throwing her hands out wide.

I laughed again and joined them in a group hug, feeling like everything was finally falling into place. I didn't have to give up ballet. I didn't have to give up Isaac. I could have the best of both worlds. My two true loves.

EPILOGUE

PEYTON

"*Y*ou did beautifully, Katelyn," I said, touching her shoulder as she ran offstage.

"Thanks, Peyton!" Katelyn grinned wide, twirling in her Clara dress for our last performance of the season.

She had come back from the Joffrey summer intensive and worked harder than I'd ever seen her over the last six months to earn this role. It had been an easy decision to make.

Bebe stood there, waiting for her. They clasped hands and jumped up and down in excitement. Bebe was already dressed in her Arabian attire, a purple fitted top and sheer purple harem pants.

Some of the professional company members were still irritated with me for giving a pre-professional dancer such an important role. The solos and *pas de deux* were usually reserved for them, but Bebe was a star. She'd already been accepted to the School of American Ballet for the summer after she graduated. I couldn't wait to see what she would do in New York. I hoped that she'd take my place one day in the New York City Ballet.

"Your cue, Beebs," I whisper-shouted.

Bebe came to stand at my side. Her poise and confidence had multiplied since I'd first started working with her.

"I can't believe this is the last show," she said to me, her dark eyes wide.

"You will perform *The Nutcracker* a thousand more times, I assure you."

"But the last with you, Peyton."

I laughed and tugged her in for a hug. "You're going to do great. Go show everyone what I knew the first moment I saw you."

"What was that?" Bebe asked.

"That you're going to rule the world."

Bebe laughed. "Fingers crossed."

"All right. In the wings."

Bebe hastened forward, took a deep breath, and said a prayer, and then she was off. As stunning as I'd ever known she would be. And I wasn't just blowing smoke. She was going to soar.

When the show ended, all the seniors cried and hugged each other. They promised to see each other again for New Year's. I spoke to each and every one of the dancers as they left backstage until I came across one of Mother Ginger's children. In the show, Mother Ginger hid the children under her skirt, and then they came out and performed a small number. The one I found was still in costume.

"Aly Cat," I said, holding my arms out.

She dashed forward and threw herself into my arms. "Peyton! I don't want *The Nutcracker* to be over."

"Me neither," I said, kissing her cheek. "But *The Nutcracker* will be here every year. What role do you think you want to play next year?"

"Sugar Plum Fairy!"

I laughed. That was always her answer. At six, she was as precocious and talented as I'd ever seen her. If she continued wanting to dance, then she could go far. But if she changed her mind and decided to be a musician or play soccer like her dad, then I was sure she would succeed there.

"How about we get you out of this costume and find your dad?"

She nodded. We quickly changed her back into jeans and a sweater and then headed hand in hand to the lobby.

Isaac stood there, looking like a dream in slacks and a red button-up, holding two bouquets of flowers. "There are my girls!"

"Daddy, Peyton said I could be Sugar Plum Fairy next year!" Aly cheered, taking the bouquet and sniffing them.

"Did she?" He arched an eyebrow as he pulled me in for a kiss. He passed me the second bouquet.

"Thank you."

"She did, Dad! I heard her."

"Well, you will have to work really hard throughout the next year to be in that role, won't you?"

"Yes." Her eyes were wide as she whirled on me. "When can I start pointe? I'll need to start practicing."

I tried to hide my grin. "When you're twelve."

Aly rolled her eyes. "That's too long. How about next week?"

I couldn't hold back my laugh this time. "I'll think about it."

"Come on, Aly Cat. Let's get you home."

"But, Dad..."

"Don't you want to open a present?" he cajoled.

"Present! Santa!"

That got her moving.

We packed Aly up into the backseat and then drove back to our house, where I knew his family and mine were waiting for us. We'd agreed they'd come over to the house to open one Christmas present. Even *Abuelita* had said she would be there. I couldn't wait to see everyone all in one place.

It had been a hard transition, moving away from New York and leaving the New York City Ballet. A part of me knew that the city and the company would always hold a place in my heart. But after I'd finished out my last two performances, I'd been glad that I'd already made the decision to leave because my knee was furious with me. When I finally got up the nerve to go to the doctor again about it, she was mad that I'd waited too long. Words like *tendon damage* and *loss of cartilage* still made me shiver at night. She'd put me in a brace and ordered six more months of PT, and things had gotten a lot better after that. Suddenly, I could dance again without pain. But likely only because I wasn't on my toes eight-plus hours a day.

Working at Lubbock Ballet Company was a dream though. There were still flaws and drama and plenty of high school angst, but Kathy hadn't lied when she said I would just fit in. I couldn't have asked for a better position.

And Isaac...well, I'd moved in as soon as I got back to Lubbock, and we'd never looked back.

"Everyone is here!" Aly yelled from the backseat.

"Surprise," Isaac said as he pulled into the garage.

I helped Aly out of her booster, and she ran toward the front door.

"Grandma!" she called as she practically attacked Isaac's mom. "Did you know I get to open a present before Santa comes?"

"I'd heard that," she said.

His mom kissed me on the cheek and then we walked inside together.

Piper and Peter stood in the foyer, passing a flask back and forth. I laughed and snatched it out of Piper's hand.

"Aren't you driving?" I asked.

"No, *Mom*," Piper said.

"Well, good," I said and then took a sip, coughing as the heat of tequila went down my throat. "Jesus!"

"Yeah, isn't it great?" Peter asked with a laugh.

"Put that away or give it to your *abuelita*," Nina said, appearing before us.

Peter looked scandalized and hid the flask.

I kissed my *abuelita* on the cheek. "I'm glad you're here."

"I made tamales for tomorrow and brought Mexican hot chocolate with me tonight. Come drink some."

I wandered into the kitchen with her to pour out the hot chocolate for people in attendance and didn't say a word as Isaac pulled down a bottle of Godiva Liqueur to add shots for the adults. I hugged my parents and said hello to Annie, who was sitting by the Christmas tree and looking through the few presents, picking them up, and shaking them, as if she could figure out what was inside.

Finally, Isaac got everyone together and held his mug up. "To our first Christmas all together. May we have many more to come!"

"Cheers!" everyone called but especially Aly, who spilled hot chocolate on the floor as she lifted her cup.

"Oops," she said into the silence.

My mom waved away Isaac's parents and found something to clean up the spill. They worked together so effortlessly. As if they had somehow known that we'd end up here. In high school, our families had spent so much time together. We'd been just one giant family, but now, we truly were all one. And it felt as if it had been meant for this moment.

Each person got one gift to open. We oohed and aahed over the presents. Aly somehow managed to open four from various people, including an art set, Barbies, hair scrunchies, and some kind of goo that I didn't understand. Isaac went over to investigate.

Then, Aly rushed over to me with a light-brown box in her hand, tied off with a red ribbon. "Peyton, it's your turn!"

"Oh, Aly, what did you get me?"

"It's a surprise!"

I took the box from her and pulled on the ribbon. It easily came away. I used it to tie a bow and place it on Aly's head. She giggled and wore it like a headband.

Then, I opened the box, finding a sea of white tissue paper within it. I removed it like a magician pulling an endless amount of fabric out of his sleeve. I laughed as the cascade fell to the ground, but my laughter stopped when I reached the bottom.

Nestled in a poof of tissue paper was a small black box. I gasped as I retrieved it from its spot and let the brown box fall away.

My eyes lifted in shock, and there was Isaac with a wide smile on his face, pleased that his surprise had worked. And everything else slipped away in oblivion. I couldn't see our families. I didn't hear Aly's excitement. I just saw the man of my dreams, standing before me, offering me the world.

Isaac took the box out of my hand and then sank to one knee. A sob escaped my lips, and my hands flew to my mouth.

"Oh my God," I whispered.

He popped open the box, revealing the circular, haloed diamond within.

"Peyton, would you do me the honor of becoming my wife?" he asked.

"Yes!" I gasped.

Tears clouded my eyes as he slipped the ring on my finger. I stared at it in amazement and then flung my arms around his shoulders. Our families cheered.

"It worked!" I heard Piper cry out.

They must have all been in on it. God, this man.

"I love you," he said against my hair.

"I love you, too."

"My turn!" Aly cried, elbowing her way in.

Isaac picked her up, and we crushed her between us.

"How do you feel about Peyton becoming part of the family?"

"Yes!" Aly said. "I want that. Peyton can be my mommy."

Isaac coughed and nodded, speechless.

"Do you think you could be my flower girl, Aly?" I asked.

She nodded. "I've watched the flowers a lot. I can definitely be a flower."

Oh, *The Nutcracker*! How it seeped into every part of our lives. I didn't even have the heart to correct her. It was too precious.

Our families came forward and congratulated us. There was another toast and hugs and kisses. And then Aly was yawning, and everyone else was heading home.

By the time Isaac and I had the house to ourselves, we were pulling out secret presents we had stashed in the top of the hall closet from Santa. I artfully arranged them under the tree. And then, when it was finished and all was quiet, he pressed a firm kiss to my lips.

"You're going to be my wife."

"Finally," I whispered, staring down at the beautiful diamond on my finger.

We'd come so far from those awkward teenagers to this moment. It hadn't been the normal route to take, but we were here, and we were together. That was what mattered.

Isaac laughed and kissed me again. "Agreed. *Finally*."

THE END

ACKNOWLEDGMENTS

The Nutcracker has always been a big part of my life. I always knew that I wanted to write a story centered around it, but then my husband and I started going to a different *Nutcracker* in a different city every year. We've seen it in Lincoln Center with the wonderful Sara Mearns as the Sugar Plum Fairy for the New York City Ballet. We saw the incredible production in San Francisco and Atlanta and Charlotte and Fort Worth and Lubbock, of course. And due to the covid, this will be the first year in nine years we don't go to a *Nutcracker* together. So, I decided to bring the *Nutcracker* to me. It was a real joy writing Peyton and the fictitious Lubbock Ballet Company into existence and to be able to donate some of the proceeds to the actual Ballet Lubbock to help the underprivileged youth have access to the arts. So thank YOU reader for helping me do just that!

Also to everyone who put their hands on this book, you're the best. Thank you to Danielle Sanchez and Maria Blalock for being sensitivity readers for the

Medina family. I wanted an authentic Mexican American experience and you helped me find it. Also to Korrie Noelle for opening a space to find sensitivity readers and helping create a more diverse and inclusive story. And Nana Malone for always inspiring me and our long talks about doing the work!

Thank you Rebecca Kimmerling, Rebecca Gibson, Anjee Sapp, Devin McCain, Kimberly Brower, Sarah Hansen, Jovana Shirley for all that you did to make this book incredible. And the audio production company Blue Nose Audio for getting the amazing Zachary Webber and Marisa Blake to bring Isaac and Peyton to life. I was so excited to get a Mexican American narrator to portray Peyton. Representation matters!

Joel, my rock, my world, my fellow lover of all things *Nutcracker*. Thanks for loving ballet almost as much as I do and insisting on traveling the world to see more and more of them! You bring me so much joy.

And of course, my mom. Thanks for paying for all of those years of dance so that I could be happy. Thanks for taking me to see the Nutcracker as a kid. And thanks for believing I could do anything I wanted, this one is for you! For your love of Christmas romance novels!

ABOUT THE AUTHOR

 K.A. Linde is the *USA Today* bestselling author of the more than thirty novels. At the age of ten, Kyla annoyed her mom enough to get into her first dance class and has never looked back. She began teaching at sixteen and has since served as the head coach of the Duke University dance team, the University of Georgia club dance team, and taught at local studios in Texas and Georgia.

She wants to bring her love of dance to all that wish to pursue it, which is why a part of the proceeds for this novel will go to promote dance education for underprivileged youth.

She currently lives in Lubbock, Texas, with her husband and two super-adorable puppies.

Visit her online:
www.kalinde.com
Facebook, Instagram, Twitter: @authorkalinde

CPSIA information can be obtained
at www.ICGtesting.com
Printed in the USA
LVHW042108021120
670484LV00008B/2006

9 781948 427432